THE QUESTING KNIGHTS OF THE FÆRIE QUEEN

Retold by

GERALDINE McCAUGHREAN

FROM THE WORKS OF EDMUND SPENSER

Illustrated by JASON COCKCROFT

Hodder
Children's
Books

A division of Hodder Headline Limited

For Ian, Victoria, Emily and William – G.McC

For Eunice - J.C.

THE QUESTING KNIGHTS OF THE FAERIE QUEEN

retold by Geraldine McCaughrean and illustrated by Jason Cockcroft

British Library Cataloguing in Publication Data
A catalogue record of this book is available from
the British Library.
ISBN 0340 86621 7 (HB)

Text copyright © Geraldine McCaughrean 2004
Illustration copyright © Jason Cockcroft 2004

The right of Geraldine McCaughrean to be identified as
the author and Jason Cockcroft as the illustrator of this Work
has been asserted by them in accordance with
the Copyright, Designs and Patents Act 1988.

First edition published 2004
10 9 8 7 6 5 4 3 2 1

Published by Hodder Children's Books
a division of Hodder Headline Limited
338 Euston Road London NW1 3BH

Printed in China

Visit Geraldine's website at www.geraldinemccaughrean.co.uk

CONTENTS

At Cleopolis,
Court of the Faerie Queen

✦ *Y*OU WON'T FIND the Land of Faerie on any atlas. It exists beyond Geography and outside Time – not Now, not Then, but somewhere in between. Its out-country can be a fearful place. Monsters spring up like weeds. Even the people out there are not all what they seem. Some of them are monsters, too.

But the Queen? Ah well, even you would recognise her, and you have never ventured over the borders of Faerie before: Gloriana is the Ideal that shines at the back of your imagination, like a gold sovereign at the bottom of a wishing well.

Cleopolis – her shining mirage of a palace – is somewhere people bring their wishes. Some arrive hoping to become a 'Queen's Knight'. Others come asking for help. And during the Queen's Festival, once a year, Gloriana despatches her knights (and would-be knights) on quests to right wrongs, rescue prisoners and slay monsters.

You came here at the right time. This year's Festival is just beginning. Minstrels, knights and courtiers are gathering under the chandeliers of dew, behind the windows of amber, among the gossamer hangings

7

and before the honeysuckle throne. Music distils out of the air like honey crystallising...

A time for stories.

Yes, yes, I hear you. You want to be a knight. Questing sounds glamorous and thrilling, doesn't it? But to be a good knight – to be a Queen's Knight? Ah...! Tell me, what does it take? Yes, yes, a lance, a sword, a shield, a good horse. But anyone can beg, borrow or steal those and still not be a knight. No. Did you know: a newly-made sword will snap if it hasn't been tempered in the fire and under the blacksmith's hammer? Knights are made the same way. And to be a knight here at Cleopolis – that takes the kind of character few possess.

There is a kind of recipe, they say – six or so sacred ingredients that make up the ideal knight: Holiness, Courage, Justice, Moderation, Love, Courtesy... more. If you or I are ever to win our knighthoods, we have to master at least some of them.

It takes pain. It costs blood – and fear and self-sacrifice. Not many can see it through. Don't take this the wrong way, but do you have any of the knightly virtues? Before you present yourself to the Queen, let me tell you about last year's quests – about the people who rode out under the Faerie banner. Forewarned is forearmed, so they say.

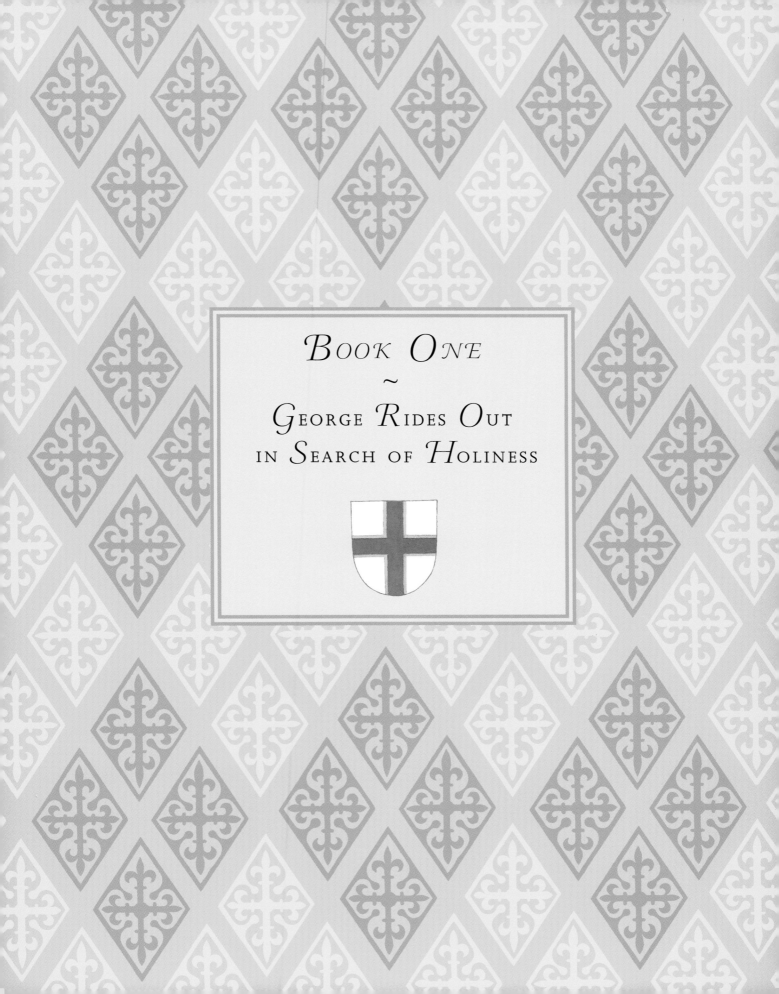

Book One
~
George Rides Out
in Search of Holiness

CHAPTER ONE
Monstrous Error and Other Big Mistakes

❧ ON THE FIRST DAY of the Festival, a great tall, gangling loon of a man arrived in Cleopolis, threw himself down in front of the Queen's throne and begged for a chance to serve her and win his knighthood. The Queen eyed him with her honey-coloured eyes, but said nothing – so he just folded up his long legs and sat down on the floor.

Within the hour, another traveller arrived: a quite different kind of person. She was dressed in white. In fact, the Princess Una was all whiteness, from the wimple encircling her face to the little donkey she tethered at the door. Her brightness, though, was masked under a black cloak, like a candle shielded within a hand. She was in mourning, you see, for happier times.

"Gracious Queen, my name is Una," she said. "My mother and father are rulers of a land far to the east of yours. But they are besieged! A huge dragon has laid siege to the castle! A vile, sickening dragon! It has laid waste to the countryside and left nothing but scorched fields and weeping!" Una's voice broke as she spoke of it, but she summoned up the courage to go on. "Some people say it can't even be killed. I won't believe that! So I escaped and came here – to Cleopolis – to fetch help! I beg you, madam – spare me one of your

11

Company of Knights – to do battle with the dragon, and save my poor parents!"

At once, the long gangling man on the floor uncoiled like a spring and burst out, "Let the quest be mine, Your Majesty! Let me prove myself! Let me kill the dragon or die trying!" A ripple of laughter ran round the room. Lords and ladies hid their smiles behind their hands.

But Queen Gloriana studied him long and hard, as though she were reading words written on his soul. "What is your name?"

"George, Your Majesty! George Redcrosse!"

"You have weapons? Armour? A shield?"

George blushed and looked down at the toes of his shabby boots.

"Very well, George Redcrosse. Equip yourself from my armoury. And remember: a dragon is Evil made flesh. And only Holiness will destroy Evil. So you must be my Quester-after-Holiness."

The laughter changed to gasps of disbelief. Entrust such a task to this scruffy stranger? He could never carry it through! Or had Gloriana's golden eyes divined something out-of-the-ordinary beneath the dust of travel, beneath the gawky awkwardness? The Court of Cleopolis studied George Redcrosse more carefully as the Queen presented him with a shield. It was not new – in fact, it was battered and buckled from use – but it was the shield of a hero; its device the blood-red cross of the Crusaders.

And what of the white-clad Una? What did she think of the Queen's choice? She had no magic to see into a man's soul. But she needed none. She had already entrusted her life to George Redcrosse. Because, in the first moment of their meeting, they had looked one another in the eye... and fallen in love.

And that is how they came to be riding – George and Una – across the plains of Faerie. George was in full armour now, sword and lance at the ready. The dents in his shield were nothing to do with him – he had never yet struck a blow in anger – but all that was about to change.

And way behind, grumbling and mumbling and stumbling along with the luggage, waddled a little knobbly tuber of a servant: Dob.

Without warning the sky turned black and, with a crack of thunder, rain teemed down. Luckily there was a wood nearby. Its leaves massed so densely that inside the wood it was dark and dry. Less luckily, the place was a maze of paths so involved and tangled that the three travellers were soon hopelessly lost. To and fro they trailed, tripping over tree roots, calling out to one another through the green gloom.

One path seemed more trodden than the rest, so they followed that until it brought them to the mouth of a dark cave. The knight was all set to go in, but the lady gave a sudden cry of alarm. "No, George! Don't! How stupid of me! I know this place! There's a monster in there – a terrible monster!"

Foreseeing his first real battle, George was more excited than alarmed. He unsheathed his sword.

"No, no! Don't be reckless, George! This is not…"

But their voices had already reached the monster, who came lumbering out into the daylight. She brought with her a stench as big as the wood. 'Error' rarely stirred out of her sty: even the green twilight of the glade pained her eyes. Seeing her blink and cringe, George thought how easy this was going to be, but he had not seen the whole of Monstrous Error.

Her great rump split into a hundred snaky tails, each armed

with a vicious sting. Scaly tentacles wound round the knight, pinning his arms, binding his legs, squeezing the air out of his lungs.

"My first adventure and I am dead meat!" thought George, and the shame was worse than the pain. It gave him the strength to pull free one arm, drag his sword from its scabbard, and strike upwards.

In answering pain, the monster spewed up frogs and toads, half-digested meat and decomposing garbage. Bizarrely there were books, too, and scrolls of paper and boots and armour. They cracked George on the head as they fell, and a bottle of red ink stained his hair red.

But there were worse things in Error's mouth. Unhinging her bag-like jaw, she let loose her babies — black, glistening worms and lizards that squirmed and knotted around the knight's feet, biting and stinging.

"Dead meat," thought George a second time, enraged by his own stupidity.

"You can do it, George!" Una's voice reached him through the pain and fear. "I believe in you!"

With one superhuman effort, George found his feet again and hacked at the monster, kicking aside her spawn. Error fell back, tried to drag herself into her dark cave, but died on the threshold.

At once, her disgusting children began to slurp up their mother's black blood — swelling up like bladders then bursting like bladderwrack on a beach.

Silence. Somewhere a bird began to sing. George's first mistake had nearly been his last. He vowed never again to fight for the sake of fighting. After all, the Lady Una was relying on him! He had no right to leave her unprotected. He had no right to risk the success of the quest! As the flies gathered, George and Una found a path out of the wood. The rain had stopped, but the sun hung low in the sky, and darkness was not far off.

Meeting the Hermit seemed like a real godsend. He came towards them along the path, a picture of holiness, lips moving in prayer.

"Please, holy father, can you tell us where we might shelter tonight?"

"My own poor cell has few comforts, but you are most welcome to them," whispered the Hermit from out of his snowy cascade of beard.

Within the hour, they had washed, and eaten a simple supper. Una spoke of her parents, besieged by the foul dragon. George spoke of his quest to kill it. "As a simple hermit of course I know nothing of the wide, wicked world,"

said the old man. "But I shall pray for you both." All evening, a haze of holy words soothed the weary travellers to the very brink of sleep. Thanking their host, they went to bed – to bare, simple chambers at opposite ends of the house. Dob the serving man watered the animals and bedded down in the stable.

Still as a plaster statue the Hermit sat, until they were all fast asleep. Then taking his floor-length beard between his teeth, he crossed the lawn to the chapel building, and his sandals slapped down stone stairs to the vault that lay beneath. There, suspended from chains like hanged criminals, dozens of books swung, their vellum pages scalloped by age. He began to read: page after page of magical symbols and unspellable words. Reaching one crooked finger high into the air above his head, he barked:

"Come sprites! Come to Archimago, Master of the Black Arts!"

From out of the eaves, a hundred small, bat-black shapes flittered. With lightning sleight of hand, the evil sorcerer plucked two out of the air and fashioned them, putty-like, between his hands…

George Redcrosse was dreaming of Monstrous Error; he woke wrestling his bedclothes. The Hermit crouched over him, long yards of beard bunching up between them. "Come quickly, knight! You must see! You ought to know what kind of lady you are serving!" He towed George over the cold stone floor, across the lawn. The lady's chamber door stood open a crack and through it came a noise of sighs and giggling. The Hermit's iron grip impelled George to look, holding his face to the gap, forcing him to spy on his lady.

There lay Princess Una… and alongside her a young man – a pretty, curly-haired, soft-lipped squire. He was kissing Una and worse – much worse – Una was kissing him back!

George broke free and ran to his room, kicking the stable door as he passed. "Dob! Wake up! Saddle my horse! We are leaving!"

Watching the two ride off into the darkness, the Sorcerer Archimago bared his teeth in a wild-man grin. For a moment, Princess Una and her young lover appeared to stand within the circle of his arms. Then he took each forgery and moulded it back into its true, flittering, bat-eared shape. As he opened his hands, the sprites flew off to roost. His beard, too, he dispensed with, wiping it from his face like soap bubbles.

"I hate you, lady," he mouthed silently through the keyhole of the bedchamber. "You with your perfect purity, dripping your spotless goodness into my eyes, like bleach. What will become of you now, abandoned by your fool of a knight?"

Then reversing his cloak, he chose a different disguise for himself from among the thousands at his command. In place of his hermit's robes he put on shiny metal, a plume, a sword, a shield. In short, he made himself into the very picture of a perfect knight.

From a distance you would have sworn you were seeing George Redcrosse.

❄ ❄ ❄ ❄ ❄ ❄ ❄ ❄ ❄ ❄

CHAPTER TWO
The Faithful and the Faithless

GEORGE HARDLY KNEW where he was or what he was doing. All he wanted was to get far away from that wanton, worthless Una. To have looked so perfect and proved so foul! How could he ever trust a woman again? And what now? Should he keep to his dragon quest, for the sake of the Faerie Queen? What dragon? Una had probably lied about that, too. And about loving him.

To the Devil with Love! thought George.

Dob, laden with luggage and struggling to keep up, dared not quibble, but kept glancing over his shoulder. He was anxious for Lady Una, and anxious for himself, alone in a strange land with this unhappy, angry knight.

Tormented by regret, George was positively glad to hear a loud, grating voice taunt him with a challenge: "Stand and fight, coward, or give me that shield of yours to scrape my boots on!"

Barring the road, mounted on a glossy stallion and magnificently accoutred, was a sallow knight in jet-black armour. Across his shield was emblazoned the one word: FAITHLESS. Behind him rode a woman dressed in purple, gem-encrusted velvet. Her horse, too, was tinselled from nose to tail: a silvery wave of fringing and plaited wire. Dazzling.

But there was no time to be dazzled, for the black knight was already advancing at a thunderous gallop. George dug in his spurs, and the two closed for combat. Like charging rams clashing skulls, the jolt was so violent that both men were stunned by it. Then Faithless swung high his sword and clipped the metal of George's helmet. A shard of metal flashed away in the sunlight. Hand-to-hand, flank against flank, they struggled, their horses circling, their knees and thighs bruising each other.

At last, rising up in his saddle, George delivered such a blow that the sallow knight's helmet cleaved open. He pitched from his horse and lay still on the ground, watching – with open, fearful, lightless eyes – his life and soul slip away. The lady made a sound like a peacock's cry.

O for the Faerie Queen to have seen that! George examined his heart for signs of new-fledged holiness. Surely destroying an evil knight was a holy act? Surely. As he went to dismount, the woman turned to flee. "Wait, lady! You are in no danger from me!" he called.

She glanced over her shoulder, eyes wide and tearful, then knelt at his feet. "I am yours now, sir. Deal kindly with me, I beg you! Life has been cruel enough to me already!"

Fidessa (she told him) was a princess – the daughter of an emperor, no less! She had been kidnapped (she said) by Faithless: "…though he could never capture my heart!" she avowed.

Then and there, Fidessa took the place of Una in George's heart, and he swore to be her champion and protector wherever their journey took them. His quest might have gone awry, but he was sure the Faerie Queen would approve. Better to serve this beautiful princess than the despicable Una!

Dob was well pleased with the way things had turned out – not because he preferred the new lady but because there was now an empty horse for him to ride.

The weather grew hotter and hotter. They entered a landscape devoid of greenery, the fierce sun flaring off flints. Two sear grey trees offered the only shade for miles around, trunks leaning against one another as if they were fainting in the heat. Fidessa and George found what shade they could under these trees. And George, in a fit of romantic ardour, tore off some twigs to twine a leafy crown for Fidessa.

A voice cried, "Stop! Have pity!" George dropped the twigs... and found his hands smeared with blood. The tree was bleeding! "Don't tear off my limbs!"

George felt the words vibrate through his back and jumped up. "Who are you? A tree sprite?"

But the poor souls trapped within the trees were no sprites. Once they had been sweethearts – happy – without a care in the world. "One day we met Duessa," said one, and the fluttering leaves of the other hissed, *Duesssa.*

"She set me a challenge: to judge who was the fairest: she or my sweetheart. I tried to compare – you know – these eyes with those eyes; that nose with this nose. But one was as lovely as the other! So that's what I said... Apparently it was the wrong answer.

"Then and there, Duessa opened her mouth and breathed out a foul, treacly, blinding fog. I could see nothing! But I could feel my skin crisping, my flesh turning solid, my eyes... When the fog cleared, here we stood, transformed into these... these..."

"Trees?" suggested Fidessa.

"Now, God help us, we stand and scorch in the sun and freeze in the frosts. And wait."

George's mouth was almost too dry to spit, but he softened some earth into mud and salved the wound in the tree's side. "Is there nothing I can do to release you from this curse?" he whispered.

"Nothing but a living well shall release us from our hell." The tree groaned its glib, sing-song doom in a voice as hollow as a rotten log.

"I'll find one! We shall make it our quest, shan't we, Fide—?" But when he turned to his lady, he saw to his horror that she lay in a dead faint.

What else could he do but carry her to her horse, then and there? All thought of healing wells and rescues was forgotten. Riding the lead horse, he failed to see how quickly Fidessa recovered from her 'swoon'. Nor did he see the triumphant sneer she flung at the twin trees.

"That voice…" one tree whispered to her mate. "That woman's voice!"

"Yes, my love," said the other desolately. "I fear Duessa has snared herself another fool."

CHAPTER THREE
The Lists of Love

*I*MAGINE THE PRINCESS Una's dismay, when she woke to find herself deserted. She was all alone, in a country swarming with wild beasts, monsters and ruffians. Worse still, the man to whom she had given her heart had ridden off with it, leaving nothing behind but a hollow pain. On her little white donkey, she could hardly hope to catch him up, but she was determined to try. Fixing her eyes on the horizon, she rode away from the hermitage and never looked behind.

So she never caught sight of the mounted rider dogging her steps.

At night she sometimes managed to beg shelter at some peasant hut, but more often bedded down under bushes or in the boles of trees. That is where she was when the lion found her.

A sweet morsel for a lion. His nostrils drizzled at the smell. His mouth drooled. In the moonlight he stood over the princess, savouring his prey.

Then the moon shone on her face – on her hand curled like a half-open lily. Una had pulled off her wimple to use as a pillow, and her golden hair fanned out across the ground.

Sometimes beasts have stronger instincts than humankind. The lion sensed such Goodness in the sleeping girl that she might as well have been fenced round with iron: his jaws simply would not close on her. Instead, when Una woke, she found the lion lying at her head like an effigy on a tomb, and knew that she had found a new escort through the barbarous world.

Of course, it is a mixed blessing to have a lion escorting you. Una saw a girl standing at a cottage door, and called: "Please! May I sleep under your roof tonight?" The girl took one look at the lion and ran indoors, slamming the door just behind her. Nothing would make her open up again.

The lion, who liked to be of help, put his paws to the door and pushed it… The girl and her grandmother had locked themselves in a cupboard and would not come out. It seemed a waste not to bed down in front of their hearth.

But in the small hours of the night, the man of the house came reeling home, drunk, from a night's banditry. He found his own front door barred against him, and no amount of shouting and swearing would persuade his mother and daughter to open up. So he fetched an axe from the woodpile and broke down the door.

He was met – to his great surprise – by a lion who pulled him limb from limb.

At first, Una, in her innocence, assumed the neighbours would be glad to be rid of such a fearful man. But in this particular barrel, one rotten apple had

soured the whole crop. The entire village resented the bandit's death, threatening Una with all manner of revenge. She fled, her donkey trembling at the knees, her black cloak billowing out behind her like a sad raincloud.

Imagine then, her joy when she saw, on the hillside ahead of her, the unmistakable figure of George Redcrosse — helmet on, visor down, cloak streaming in the wind. "Oh George! I have found you at last!"

She did not harken back to the hermitage or the troubles George had caused her. Una was as full of forgiveness as a hive is of sweetness. She was with her escort again, and past wrongs evaporated. So she did not ask why he had left her, and she spoke no word of reproach.

The rider spoke no word either — of any kind — which was strange.

The lion sniffed the air, a little puzzled, then fell into step behind them both — a golden shadow padding over sunlit grass.

Suddenly, there was a fourth figure: a brown knight on a sweat-streaked stallion, barring the way. "Stand and fight, sir knight! You killed my brother Faithless, and I mean to make you pay!"

"I did?" said the Red-Cross Knight.

"You killed this man's brother?" asked Una turning to her knight.

"No! I... I mean..." said the Red-Cross Knight. (If he had done, he certainly seemed to have forgotten.) The avenging knight charged, foam flying from his own and his horse's lips. His lance point struck the Red-Cross Knight in the chest, lifting him out of the saddle and sending him sprawling on his back amid the ferns.

Una's heart seemed to stop. Had she come all this way, only to see her champion killed before her eyes? Jumping down from the donkey, she ran to his side — but the brutal brown knight got there first, snatching up the red-and-white shield and ripping off the helmet.

A quantity of grey seemed to spill out of the fallen knight's head. Both girl and villain fell back with a cry. For young George Redcrosse had apparently aged fifty years! A long grey beard unravelled down his bloody chest and his deathly-white face was as shrivelled as a walnut.

"The Hermit?" cried Una.

"Archimago?" cried the brown knight.

For a dreadful, icy moment victor and victim regarded each other in silence… Then the lion pounced. The dark knight threw up his shield, stuck out his sword – and the great cat fell limply to the ground.

Though barely conscious, Archimago heard Una's sobbing screams and his pale lips parted in a smile of satisfaction; at least she would continue to suffer – if not at his hands, then at the hand of a pitiless world.

The brown knight rode off and Una was left alone in the roadway, her white dress fluttering like a flag of surrender.

❄ ❄ ❄ ❄ ❄ ❄ ❄ ❄ ❄ ❄ ❄

CHAPTER FOUR
Pride Before a Fall

MEANWHILE THE WITCH Duessa was leading an unsuspecting George towards a distant glimmer of towers. She called it House Magnificent.

"Is it your father's home? The Emperor's?"

"Oh no, no. But you'll like it. It befits a man of your… quality," she said.

Its breathtaking splendour made him gape. The broad avenues were a-flutter with banners and pennants, and every road crowded with people in holiday clothes. They waved at George and whispered to each other that he must be the hero of some great victory. Some even broke out clapping. It was all very flattering.

George and 'Fidessa' were entertained like royalty. They slept between silken sheets in a room of sumptuous elegance. At one point Fidessa cried out in her sleep: "Win, bold knight, and you win my heart!" George smiled; she must be reliving his fight with that villain Faithless. He lay back, remembering – cut – slash – lunge! If only the Faerie Queen could have seen it!

Just once, he turned over and saw tears crawl from under Fidessa's sleeping lashes. And when she spoke in her sleep, she got his name wrong…

"Oh Faithless! Faithless, my love!"

…but then people say the oddest things in dreams.

"Master! Master, wake up!" It was not Fidessa at his side but Dob, and he
was dragging the blankets off the bed, pushing the boots on to
George's feet. "Get up, Master! We have to get out of
here! I went for a scout around, and you don't want
to know what I found!"

Exploring the palace, Dob had found his way
down to the dungeons. There, crammed in too
tightly to draw deep breath, lay hundreds of
prisoners – the living in among the dead –
condemned to everlasting imprisonment. The
jaunty plumes of their helmets had been
chewed away by rats. Women, in gowns of satin
and velvet, sprawled on dirty straw. Scholars,
academics, poets and musicians were burning
vellum pages for the sake of light and warmth.
All those still alive were bemoaning the vanity
that had brought them to this hell-hole. "Why did
we listen to her lies and her flattery?" they wept.
"Why did we put ourselves in her power?"

"Where is the Lady Fidessa?" George asked Dob.
"We must get out of here at once! Tonight!" Dob
shrugged. George did not want to leave without his lady – it
put him painfully in mind of leaving Una – but Dob picked him up bodily and
ran for the stables. Hanging head-down over Dob's shoulder, George began to
see things… differently.

The hangings on the stairs were not cloth-of-gold at all, but sacking
painted yellow! The gems set into the walls were not emeralds and rubies but
coloured glass. The gilding on the pillars was all peeling away, revealing worm-
eaten rotten wood underneath. In fact, the great citadel was one gigantic piece
of stage scenery held together with string and lies.

Dob threw saddles on to their horses.

"But I cannot leave without my lady!" protested George.

"She'll follow, master."

So they crept out of the city at dawn. The first rays of the sun picked out

25

words carved over the portcullis – not 'House Magnificent', but THE HOUSE OF PRIDE.

'Fidessa' returned to the perfumed, silken bedroom, the hem of her dress scorched and a faint whiff of sulphur in her hair. Seeing the empty bed, she gave a shriek. Had George slipped through her fingers while she was gone?

She should not have let him out of her sight... and yet she had had to go. She had had to clamber down to Hell and haggle with the Devil for the soul of her dear dead lover, Faithless. Duessa gave a sob of frustration: her journey had proved fruitless – the Devil had denied her – and now George had escaped! Vexation! She would have to go after him.

He was easy to find. He had gone only as far as the woodland fountain before stopping to wait for her. 'Fidessa' flung her arms around him: "Never run off like that again, my love! I thought you had abandoned me! How would I live without my beloved knight!" George was very glad of her soft hands ruffling his hair. "Rest," urged Fidessa. "Let me fetch you water from that fountain. I happen to know it has magical properties."

"Of Holiness?" asked George remembering, for some reason, the Faerie Queen's words: Only Holiness will destroy Evil..."

"Mmmm," said Fidessa. "Something like that."

George loosed his breastplate. They had escaped the House of Pride! Surely it was safe to drop his guard now and just revel in being alive? The water from the fountain was very cold; after drinking it, an odd sickness sat on his stomach. He closed his eyes...

Then dead pine needles were jumping on the forest floor. Acorns fell from the oaks. Something big was coming! George reached for his sword – but his hands felt heavy as lead, his head as big as a boulder. It took all his strength even to get to his knees. "What's wrong with me?" he asked, but his speech slurred. Still Fidessa smiled – not at him now, but past him. When he followed her gaze, he had his first sight of... Orgoglio.

A great bloated mountain of flesh came wobbling and flapping like a marquee full of wind, an oak tree grasped in one hand, its roots dripping soil. Orgoglio used the tree for a club. Though George stumbled aside, the mere draught knocked him flat. He had no more strength to run than a newborn baby. The next stroke would crush him.

"Don't!" It was Fidessa's voice. The giant hesitated. George whimpered with gratitude. Fidessa would persuade the giant to spare him! Sweet, Fidessa! "Don't kill him, Orgoglio," Duessa said. "Stow him in your castle dungeon. You and I can have fun tormenting him." Swaying her hips, loosing her plait, toying with the hairs on the giant's sweating palms, she whispered softly: "You see this gutted herring here? You would never think it to look at him, but he killed my darling Faithless."

Suddenly Una's bright whiteness burned a hole in George's memory, and he heard the voice of his conscience loud and clear. It was not Una who had duped him, but the Hermit and this vicious creature here.

"A quick death is too good for him," Duessa was saying. "Give me this mouse to play with, Orgoglio, and I'll be your own little pussycat. Well? Duessa is yours if you want her."

After they had gone — after George had

been flung, limp and helpless, over Orgoglio's back, and giant and witch had gone giggling on their way, Dob came out of hiding. He could hardly stifle his sobs as he gathered up the scattered pieces of armour. He could barely shape his lips into a whistle, but the horse came, even so. Dob hung the armour on to George's empty saddle.

What to do? What could a little chap like Dob do, all on his own, except go in search of help – someone willing to mount a rescue mission to the Castle of Orgoglio.

But where in all the round, deceitful world was such a man to be found?

❊　❊　❊　❊　❊　❊　❊　❊　❊　❊　❊

Chapter Five
To the Rescue

Dob did not find help, but he did find Una. She stood on the edge of a wood surrounded by prancing fauns – creatures no bigger than muntjac deer but alarmingly strange. Dob ran forward, shouting.

The fauns jumped and capered about. "We'll save you, lady!" they cried, hiding behind her with their eyes tight shut.

"Calm yourselves, little ones," she told them. "It is just Dob – dear, faithful Dob!"

Wandering the world with no lion and no knight to defend her, Una had wandered into this green territory of the fauns. Luckily, their yellow, slanting eyes could judge between good and bad. Just as the lion had sniffed out her perfection, the fauns and satyrs spied Una's matchless goodness.

Now, Dob began to gabble to Una of witches and giants and dungeons and of rescuing George Redcrosse. But Una interrupted him. "Why are you telling me these lies, Dob?" she said. "Do you think I don't know? A priest passed through the wood yesterday. He told me. He saw it with his own eyes: a pack of wolves killing George. My lovely champion is dead."

"Well, your priest was either short-sighted or lying!" said Dob obstinately. "Probably Archimago the Sorcerer up to his old tricks! George Redcrosse will die, right enough, if we don't go and rescue him, but he ain't dead yet!"

"Tell me," said Una.

"You won't like it, lady…"

"Tell me anyway."

And so Dob recounted the whole unsavoury story – why George had abandoned her at the hermitage; how he had fallen into the clutches of Duessa and Orgoglio. "He's let you down, lady, and that's a fact."

"He's alive, Dob, and that's all that matters. A moment ago I thought he was dead, but he's alive! Now… which way to this castle?" Una might look as palely fragile as a lighted candle, but it took more than a witch and a giant to make her abandon George.

The fauns wept and herded together in grief. "Stay with us! Stay with us!" they pleaded. But Princess Una kissed each one then mounted up among the fragments of George's armour, and Dob led the way back towards the Castle of Orgoglio. What such a pair could do to rescue their knight, God alone knew, but they had to try.

Watching from his hiding place, Archimago cursed. Like a fat black inkblot, the sorcerer kept trying to put an end to the story of George Redcrosse, and somehow this woman foiled him every time. Still, what could she do – what could anyone do? No one had ever escaped the Castle of Orgoglio. Those particular dungeons were the deepest and direst in the whole dark world.

Like sunset before the dark, the Golden Knight appeared in their path, breathtaking – magnificent. Una and Dob gasped at the sight of him. His dazzling armour was gold, set with gemstones, and inset into his breastplate – directly over his heart – was a portrait of the Faerie Queen. He was accompanied by his squire, and mounted on a horse as prancing as sea surf.

Was this another of Archimago's disguises?

"Why is your shield covered, sir? Most knights are proud to declare their heraldry," said Una.

He glanced down at the cloth draped over his buckler. "It is for the best. Trust me."

"He never uncovers it – wouldn't dare! It's too—" began the squire, but was hushed by a single finger lifted in his direction.

"This is my squire, Timian," said the knight. "A good boy. His nature is almost as open as his mouth… and he will do his part, I'm sure, when we reach Orgoglio's Castle."

Dob stared. "You are going to help us?"

"Naturally. Your knight cannot hope to save himself." And without more ado, he turned his horse's head and fell in beside stallion and donkey. Una's heart rose to think that such a knight was now fighting in her cause.

Orgoglio's Castle was vast and forbidding. Its moat and motte were strewn with filth and bones, and the gates were shut fast.

"Timian, blow your horn," said the Golden Knight to his squire.

The boy sounded one brash, blaring, magical note. The iron-studded gates burst outwards as though explosive charges had been set behind them, and promptly sank into the slime of the moat.

Out came Orgoglio, the ground quaking under his feet. Gross and gruesome, he was, caped in sweaty blubber and the stench of evil.

His consort, riding in his wake, proved still more shocking. For Orgoglio had mounted the Lady Duessa on a monstrous, seven-headed beast – each head with a lick of fire for a tongue, a mouthful of half-eaten meat and a tawdry, tinny crown. Duessa, too, was decked out in every kind of gaudy finery.

The giant came at the Golden Knight wielding his leafless tree for a club. With every blow, its tip sank into the ground, deep as a grave. It shook the knight's horse off its feet, but the champion was quickly back on his feet, undaunted, nimbly dodging the rain of blows, hacking at the giant with a blade as bright as lightning.

One such blow struck off Orgoglio's left arm. Seeing her lover wounded, Duessa set her monstrous beast at the Golden Knight. It came ramping down on him – seven heads all hungry for his blood. Even the bravest of men cannot fight two such foes at the same time!

Timian, seeing his master's plight, hurled himself in the path of the charging beast.

But Duessa only doused him from her golden drinking cup, with a noxious potion of poison and magic. It stole the very marrow out of the boy's bones leaving him weak as water. One of the beast's clawed paws grappled him round the neck and, if the Golden Knight had not broken away from Orgoglio to strike off one monstrous head, his squire would have been torn apart and shared between seven mouths.

Wounded, the seven-headed beast pitched and staggered. Duessa was thrown from its back, but Orgoglio came to her aid, swinging the club, catching the Golden Knight a blow that jarred all the breath from his lungs. He went down, pole-axed.

"Dead! Dead! Down and dead!" triumphed the giant.

But the blow had dislodged the cloth covering the knight's shield. Snagged on a splinter of Orgoglio's club, it lifted clear now. The shield was not metal at all, but diamond, polished to a blinding brightness! The sunlight pierced the giant's eyes, singeing his brain, stunning him so that he reeled on his heels. The seven-headed beast, too, stood stock still, blinded, rocking. Recovering his breath, the Golden Knight picked up his sword, dragged himself to his feet… and struck.

Orgoglio burst. Like a tent collapsing to the ground, he deflated. Then his very substance disappeared, like water soaking into the ground and there was nothing left but a dirty stain.

Duessa tried to slink off, but her gaudy robes and glinting finery gave her away. "Seize her, Timian!" called the Golden Knight. "We shall deal with her when we have found our man!"

The Castle of Orgoglio was a hollow treasure house. Gorgeous, gilded rooms echoed with emptiness: no sign of life but for one old man who came shuffling out of the shadows clutching a bunch of keys. He wore his head back-to-front as if refusing to see what stared him in the face.

"Which way to the dungeons?" Una begged him.

"Dunno!" groaned the old man. "Dunno nothing, me."

"Where is my master?" demanded Dob.

"Dunno!" the old man repeated. "Dunno nothing, me. Blind Ignoramus dunno nothing!"

The Golden Knight wrenched the keys from the old man's belt and plunged into the bowels of the Castle. It was a hell-hole. Each wall crawled with spidery regret and sticky webs of despair. The door hinges screamed in torment and the stench of sin was knee-deep. The Golden Knight strode down each foul corridor throwing open doors with a clang like the tolling of a bell.

At last, in the tiniest, foulest, deepest dungeon of all, without one thread of light, they found George Redcrosse. At first sight he seemed dead, face down in the filth, shackled hand and foot. But to his own disgust and sorrow, George was alive. The light from the open door made him cover his eyes, draw up his legs against his chest and weep.

Una rushed to his side – as though to some glittering knight fresh from jousting – and washed his face with her tears. To her, this was the same dear George to whom she had given her heart. Her faith in him never wavered. But he responded with no glimmer of relief or happiness. "Don't make me go out there!" he whispered. "The daylight will shine right through me!"

Out in the yard, he suffered the light like a man being shot through with arrows. He was skin and bone, his eyes sunk so deep into his head that he looked like a skull.

The Golden Knight gave orders that Duessa should be stripped of her gorgeous robes. And out from under the finery emerged a hag so hideous, so foully scabby that she sickened all who saw her.

George, though, did not look away. He was teaching himself how Falsehood looks: Falsehood and Deceit and Treachery, so that he would never again be taken in by it.

And when he compared himself with Una – when he looked back on his abysmal quest – he found himself far uglier than the foul Duessa.

❄ ❄ ❄ ❄ ❄ ❄ ❄ ❄ ❄ ❄ ❄

Chapter Six
A Dream of Arthur

"WHO ARE YOU? Why did you risk your life to help us?" The Golden Knight seemed to deliberate for a moment, studying Una, wondering whether to confide in her his name. "Have you heard of Arthur, one-time King of Albion? Ah – I see you have. Even here in Faerie Land, eh? I wonder what fragments of my story have blown here on the wind. Merlin? Excalibur? The Round Table? Well, you mustn't believe everything… Legends are like trees – they grow with the centuries. But you may have heard how Arthur fell wounded in his last battle and was rowed across to magic Avalon to be healed."

Una nodded, spellbound, dumbstruck.

"That part of the story is true. It is true, too, that Arthur lives on, sleeping the centuries away, awaiting the day Albion has need of him again." The Golden Knight hesitated, almost shyly, laying his hand tenderly over the portrait on his breast. "Well... sleepers dream. In my magic sleep, I dreamt of a queen more beautiful than any in Albion. And in my dreams I set out for Faerie Land, determined to serve that most perfect of ladies... And my dreaming brought me here."

"You are Arthur?" breathed Princess Una. The Golden Knight looked at her with Celtic eyes. He did not deny it.

"You're in love with the Faerie Queen?" Dob snorted with laughter. "You and every other knight!"

"My heart is hers; my sword is hers to command," said Arthur simply. "And since George here is one of her Company, it's my duty to help him. Even so... Timian and I must be on our way. George is the prisoner of Despair just now, but soon he will escape. Soon he will be equal to his quest, and the glory must be all his. In time, I suspect he will come to be far greater than Arthur of Albion ever was... Come, Timian! To Cleopolis!"

Una stared after them, wrestling with the notion of a dreaming king, a dream hero, a knight with all the perfection of youth and the wisdom of old age. Could this truly be the Arthur of legend, dreaming himself a new and marvellous quest in the realm of Faerie? Such was his splendour that she wondered if she was the one dreaming.

But George scarcely lifted his head to watch Arthur gallop away. He sat slumped in his saddle, as wretched as if he were still in that lightless dungeon. He despised himself. As a questing knight, he had failed at every turn. He had deserted Una, succumbed to Duessa's lies, to the sin of Pride, and to Orgoglio. He would never be able to forgive himself. "I wish I were dead," he mumbled, hand straying to his dagger.

And Una slapped him.

"What are you thinking of, man? Just because YOU can't forgive yourself, do you seriously think GOD can't! Wake up! Think of your quest! Think of my poor parents besieged by the dragon! They're relying on you, George! Why are you wasting time here?"

George blinked and shook his head. He looked at the dagger in his hand and could not think how it had got there. "I've got a dragon to kill!" he cried and, spurring on his horse, he galloped away. Una stared for a moment at her tingling palm, remounted and trotted after him.

So at last George Redcrosse reached the lands of Princess Una – a scorched and blasted waste scattered with the ruins of buildings and the graves of brave men. Many had fought the dragon that besieged Una's home, but none had lived to speak of it. Sealed up in their brass tower, Una's parents looked out on a realm reduced to ashes.

But George was no longer afraid. Here was the challenge granted him by the Faerie Queen! Here was the feat for which his mistakes and sufferings had prepared him! He buckled on his armour with its blood-red blazon. He closed up the visor of his plumed helmet. He took up his red-cross shield and bright sword. Among his weapons, too, were Love, Faith and the Wisdom of Experience. He had even learned to forgive himself. In short, he had discovered something of Holiness.

The question remained, were his stocks of Holiness great enough to snuff out the dragon's fire?

Its meat was human flesh; its delight was pain; its only emotion Hate. Armoured from snout to tail in brass scales, it sported wings like pirate sails, a tail bristling with poisonous stings, and its long throat sang with heat, like the flue above a furnace. At the sight of a knight, it came scurrying out, still chewing on its last kill.

All day they fought, the knight nimbly dodging, lunging and hacking at the brass-mailed beast, trying to find some weak spot through which his blade might enter. Sulphur charred his hair and soot smeared his heraldry. But time and again he ran in under the monstrous body to stab and slash. At last he found a soft armpit and dealt the beast a wound that made it howl.

His reward was a firestorm that turned his armour into a searing sheath of red-hot metal. Trapped within it, George felt his skin blister and his clothes burst into flame. The dragon dismissed him with one rap of its brass wing, and he was falling – screaming and falling – down a grassy slope and into a pocket of merciful dark.

Una screamed, too, believing she had just seen her knight burned to death. She fell on her knees and prayed – a wordless prayer, a prayer without beginning or end, a prayer that outlasted the rising of the moon. Then she ran to the place where he had fallen. And there, floating face down in a pool of icy water, lay her love.

By first light, the dragon came back, scurrying along on its crooked legs, hungry for the burned body of his victim. But up rose George to meet him, sword at the ready. His fall had plunged him, you see, into the icy Well of Life, healing his burns, blessing him for his courage.

All day they fought, George nimbly swerving and feinting to avoid the claws and teeth, trying to find some weakness in the beast's hide. The ground on which they fought became bald of grass and sodden with blood. At last, a claw as large as a tree root scythed past the knight's head and George parried. Down fell the claw – severed from its paw – and the dragon let out another yowl of agony.

It let fall, too, a spew of filthy smoke, chokingly toxic, that made George stagger backwards, fighting for breath. Losing his footing in the churned mud, he slipped and fell, sliding downhill to collide, in a bone-shivering thud, with the trunk of a tree. Rosy fruit rattled down on to the charred plumes of his helmet.

Una screamed, fell on her knees and prayed – a wordless prayer, a prayer without beginning or end, a prayer that outlived the rising of the moon and its setting, too. Then she ran to where her knight lay, thinking to find him as spoiled as a windfall apple.

But the tree too had been pierced, and down from its trunk ran a torrent of sap on to the man at its feet, bathing him in magic. For George lay at the foot of the Tree of Life and its outstretched branches were blessing him for his perseverance.

By first light, the dragon came back, hungry for the broken body of its victim. But up rose George to meet it, sword drawn, energy renewed.

All day they fought, George circling and slashing, goading and grappling in a struggle to the death. Wearying of this puny adversary, the dragon opened its jaws to swallow him down…

That was when George struck. The cavernous dragon's mouth gaped, and George struck home at the dark, soft interior. The dragon choked and fell. Its scaly flank crashed against the base of a high brass tower. Fire out, scales dull, it shuddered and died.

Turning his face to the sky in search of breath, George saw a man and woman peeping down at him from a small window at the very top of the tower. George steadied himself and bowed. "Sire! Madam! The Court of the Faerie Queen greets you! May I take this opportunity to ask for your daughter's…"

But then, somehow, exhaustion got the better of him and he slid down the wall into a deep and dreamless sleep.

❊　❊　❊　❊　❊　❊　❊　❊　❊　❊

CHAPTER SEVEN
Holy Joy

THE COUNTRYSIDE CAME alive again — with flowers and crops, birds and blossom. The wedding was an occasion for dancing in the fields, weaving flowers into circlets and baking new bread. Everyone wanted to see their princess married to her heroic knight. Red-and-white flags cracked at the head of every flagpole. The church door was strung with white and red roses. Music played night and day, because the dragon was dead. Every street was lined with well-wishers who said of the bride and groom that they had never seen two people more in love.

Then a messenger came with a letter. He picked his way through the congregation and, bowing low, handed a parchment to the King. The King's eyes had grown old and he handed it to the Queen. She looked over the inky tangle of letters. "Stop! This wedding cannot happen!"

The congregation shifted on its knees and murmured their dismay. Una picked up the letter and lifted her veil to read it. (Her black cape was gone now, and she was all whiteness.) She read:

"Beware! This knight is not free to marry. He is already betrothed. No matter what he says, George Redcrosse is betrothed to ME. For the love of honour, do not proceed. No happiness can come from a marriage founded on lies!

Yours, in grief, the Lady Fidessa."

The King and Queen drew closer to one another, aghast. George read over Una's shoulder. Then they faced one another.

Both knew the truth now, when they saw it. And that's why both of them burst out laughing!

"Archimago!"

"Who else?"

There was a scuffling and the messenger bolted down the aisle, leaping over prayer stools, tripping over guests.

"Shut the door!" called George, and the church doors swung in the impostor's face. "Up to your old tricks again, Archimago? Did you really think your lies could come between Una and I? You poor fool."

The sorcerer cursed and recovered his true shape – decidedly battered and bedraggled after his long campaign of hatred. His dirty hair and beard were like the stuffing escaping from a frayed old cushion. Wound in chains and shackled hand and foot, he was bundled into a dark dungeon beneath the brass tower. By the end of the day he was forgotten. All that mattered was that George the Dragon-Slayer and his

Lady Una had completed their fearful quest and won through to happiness!

Outside the city, the dragon's carcass melted away like a bonfire burned down to its ashes, and left nothing but a reminder of itself in every blood-red sunset.

First they took water from the Well of Life to those twin trees languishing in the desert. Then George and Una rode on to Cleopolis to beg the blessing of the Faerie Queen.

No one laughed now at the sight of George Redcrosse, that man of small beginnings. "You have my blessing," said the Queen, sword resting on George's shoulder. "But answer me three questions, now that your quest is complete. First tell me: what is a knight?"

"A knight is a buffer between the Wicked and the Helpless," said George.

"And what is Holiness?"

"A cloak to keep out the chill of Evil," said George.

Her eyes were sharp and probing – fearful to a lesser man. "Lastly tell me – who defeated the dragon?"

George spoke without hesitation. "God defeated the dragon, Your Majesty. I was only the gauntlet He put on."

The bright sword flexed. "Then arise, Sir George, Knight of Holiness, and may God bless you wherever your quests take you in the world."

Una started. Perhaps she had thought her husband's days of danger were over. But she said nothing. Courtesy in all things, here at Cleopolis.

And knighthood is not a matter of one quest. That's only the beginning.

I hear Archimago escaped. Still out there, making mischief. Every time you think he's dead or safely out of the way, up he pops again.

Wickedness is like that.

Book Two

~

Guyon Rides Out by Way of the Golden Mean

CHAPTER ONE
Fire, Water and Gold

ON THE SECOND day of the Festival, a pilgrim called Palmer, footsore and leaning heavily on his staff, arrived at Cleopolis with a dreadful story to tell. On his way back from the Holy Land, he had sighted an island — a rootless, wandering island. Woven from stranded magic, it had been nailed together with spells by a witch named Acrasia. Now she sat in her magical garden like a spider in its web, luring in passers-by.

The passers-by were never seen again!

"As far as I can gather," said Palmer with a shudder of disgust, "the delights of the island sap a man's will to leave. And once Acrasia has snared him, her magic… changes him."

"Changes him? How, 'changes him'?" asked the Queen, leaning forward in her amber throne.

"Into… into… a wild beast." A gasp of horror ran round the Great Hall.

At the back of the room, Sir Guyon overturned his bench as he jumped to his feet. Red hair on end, fist banging the furniture, he begged the Queen, "Let me go and destroy this witch and her snare!"

"Peace, Guyon. Calm yourself," said the Queen, picking real flowers from the embroidered garden of her spreading skirts. "If you want it so badly, the quest is yours. But take Palmer with you — and go carefully. There are things to be learned on such a quest, and unless you learn them, you won't come back to us. Take Palmer's advice. Take the Middle Way. You must be my 'Knight of the

Golden Mean'." And threading the flowers through the buttonhole of his jerkin, she touched him lightly on the forehead. "Speed well," she said — though she might just have been naming the flower.

Guyon yelped with delight. Here was his chance to outdo, overcome, excel! Time to throw caution to the wind and ride full tilt for adventure!

A mile down the road, he burst out impatiently, "All right! I give in! Tell me what it is. What is the Golden Mean? How do you spell it? Mien as in 'face'? Mean as in 'miser'? What does it mean?"

"It means you must steer a middle course," said Palmer in soothing, fatherly tones. "Like the child in the story: not too hot, not too cold; not too hard, not too soft; not too high, not too low."

Guyon bulged his eyes in outraged scorn; just how old did Palmer think he was? Six? "You mean she wants me to be ordinary? Middle-of-the-road? Mediocre?"

"My dear young man," said Palmer smoothly. "If you prove mediocre in any way, we are both as good as dead."

A page in orange livery came dashing down the road, waving his arms over his head. "Take cover! Hide! Get off the road! My master's coming!"

"Why? Who is your master?" asked Palmer.

"They call him The Firebrand!" hissed the page in a stage whisper. "And if you get the wrong side of his temper — ooh sir, I'm telling you — you won't even live to regret it!" Then jabbing a penknife into Guyon's knee for no apparent reason, he ran off again at top speed.

Guyon rubbed his knee and contemplated the knight riding towards him. He was dressed from head to foot in fiery red, as if his bad temper had heated his armour red-hot from the inside. On his shield were the words: *I burn and am burned.*

Without word of a challenge or grievance, Firebrand levelled his lance and charged, but Guyon was ready. He swerved aside, then lowered his own lance to meet the second charge.

"Remember, Guyon!" called Palmer. "Never fight in anger!" (Strange thing to say when someone is trying to murder you.)

Firebrand's face turned purple with rage, eyes screwed almost shut, teeth grinding so loudly that Guyon could hear them above the snort of the horses. He had enormous strength but absolutely no self-control, heaving and hacking, swiping and slashing, as if he were hewing his way through dense, hated jungle. So this is what Palmer had meant! Guyon had only to keep a cool head, duck the blows and land hit after hit upon the fiery-red armour. When, within a minute, Firebrand landed on his back in the mud, Guyon spared his life, saying, "With a temper that bad, you have problems enough already, sir."

Palmer beamed with delighted approval.

Finding himself unhorsed and – worse still – spared by this whippersnapper elf-knight, Firebrand was consumed with rage. After Guyon and Palmer had ridden off, he ran to a nearby pond and threw himself in. But there was just too little water either to drown him or to put out his sizzling rage. He found himself sitting up to his waist in muddy water, punching the waves into spray. It was a while before he even heard the man on the bank calling to him.

"Give me your hand. Let's get you out. I have just the ointments to heal those hurts of yours…"

It was Archimago the Sorcerer.

Guyon too had reached water. He and Palmer stood at the edge of a wide river, wondering how to cross over. Then a ferryboat slid from under a nearby willow, a lovely young woman at the oars. "Shall I row you across?" she asked in a husky enchanting voice.

No sooner was Guyon aboard than the boat moved out from the shore, leaving Palmer stranded. "Hey! What about my companion?"

She gave a sleepy shrug.

"Remember where we are going!" called Palmer. (Strange words from a man who has just missed the boat.)

They skimmed through the dangling curtain of willow – and Guyon found himself not on a river at all but on a wide muddy lake, no bank in sight. "Just where are you taking me?" he demanded, trying to stand up.

"For a rest, that's all," she soothed him. "Everyone needs to rest. Kiss me, knight."

"Thank you all the same, but… if you would just row me where I asked… I'm on an important quest."

"Why do you knights want to go questing after an early death? Give it up! Stay with me. No worries. No danger. An easy life. Give me a kiss."

"Ah well… ahem. Better not. My heart is, in fact, ahem… well, for some time… you know… spoken for."

"Kiss me anyway," she said, shipping her oars.

Guyon had to admit he was tempted. She was a great beauty and her breath was sweet. The sun was warm, the island inviting… But Palmer's words nudged irritatingly in his head: *Remember where we are going.* He made a grab for one of the oars. The girl grabbed the other. They both paddled and splashed in opposite directions. The boat spun.

"Look here… don't want a rest!" Guyon panted. "Just want… cross the river… go on my way. Don't want a lady. Don't need a lady! Just my quest!"

"All right, all right. No need to be insulting." Terse and frosty-faced, the girl tugged the oar out of his hand. Then she rowed him through a second curtain of willow leaves and on… to the exact point on the riverbank he had wanted to reach. She did not say goodbye. When he asked her to fetch Palmer over too, she ignored him, heading back, tugging hard on the oars.

So Guyon was on his own! On foot now, he struck off through the trees. He would just have to complete his quest without Palmer — but that was all right. He had never understood why the Queen had wanted that glum, ageing pilgrim to tag along.

When he first heard the tinkling, Guyon mistook it for running water or a horse's bridle. But when he came to the clearing he found a much stranger sight. An old man, dressed in filthy rags, squatted by something the size of a charcoal burner's mound. But this mound was not of turf but money! The tinkling had been coins trickling through the old man's fingers as he gloated over his hoard. When he saw Guyon, he made no attempt to hide or pocket his treasure. On the contrary: "Come closer, come close, my dear," he said. "Help yourself, won't you?"

"It's yours," said Guyon. A feeling of deep uneasiness crept down his shirt collar like a handful of beetles.

"Nonsense! Plenty for all. Take some. I'm sure you can find a use for it. Nobody ever has enough money in this world."

Guyon stepped closer. "Is it stolen? A man of honour can't afford to…"

"Oh don't worry on that account!" said the old man jumping up with surprising agility. "It's all fresh minted. Gold from my mines. Newly cut from the earth. Come and see Mammon's Mines. That's me. Mammon the Millionaire."

He drew Guyon by the arm, along woodland paths and on to a plain. Overhead, all manner of black birds gathered, wingspans wide as a man's cloak. They shut out the daylight, masked out the sun. Narrower and narrower the ravine grew, until the pathway plunged down into dank, dark rock. The clang of picks and hammers was loud enough to drive out all thought.

A hundred thousand people were grubbing gold from the rocks, piling it up in mounds of ore. "Help yourself! Do! It's yours!" said Mammon.

"I'm sure there are people who need it far more than I do," said Guyon.

"Plenty for everyone, my dear," Mammon insisted.

Though the light was dim, Guyon thought he could see, near every pile of money, some beast down on its haunches, ready to spring. "I prefer to travel light, thank you," said Guyon. "I'm on foot now."

"You have pockets! I'll send for a barrow! Just think, my dear, what a barrowful of gold could buy – a horse for one thing! A quiet life, a well-born wife, the adoration of your friends…"

"I have enough for my needs, thank you," said Guyon. Nearby, something gave a sharp whine.

They came to a great hall – vast and magnificent – crammed with people busy at their prayers. Guyon could see no kind of altar. Instead, the devout worshippers seemed to be paying homage to a young woman sitting on a burnished throne.

"My daughter," said Mammon, waggling his fingers in her direction. She does have a great many admirers, as you can see." Suddenly he slapped Guyon on the back. "But do you know what, my boy? I've taken such a shine to you that I believe you should have her! What do you say? You won't find a bigger dowry anywhere, and that's the truth!"

Guyon blushed pinkly: "…kind… I'm sure… but I'm already… you know… suited." He could almost hear Palmer saying, *Too much, too much.*

The Mines of Mammon seemed to extend clear through the bowels of the world. Mile after mile they walked. Guyon lost all track of time. Day and night made no difference to the plight of the miners, shovelling their precious litter into glittering mounds. The old man's pets gained in courage until they were sniffing Guyon's heels.

At last Mammon and Guyon came to an orchard (of sorts). Two trees ripe with golden fruit overarched a chair of exquisite filigree silver.

"Pick the fruit, my dear! Sit and rest yourself! See the craftsmanship of the chair? Exquisite! All these years it has stood here awaiting you. You are a man who would wear wealth well, my dear! Believe me, I'm a judge of these things."

"Very pretty, I'm sure," said Guyon, "but I'm not tired just now, thank you." He swayed, dizzy with fatigue, too weary to place one foot in front of the other. And so, for a long time they simply stood, admiring the silver throne, Mammon pressing Guyon to sit, Guyon politely declining. There was no noise but for the beasts breathing and snuffling, the tinkling of the metal leaves, the chirrup of artificial songbirds.

All of a sudden, Mammon gave a grunt – somewhere between a growl and a curse – and set off again through the long, low corridors. He walked quickly now, so that Guyon stumbled and tripped along in his wake. A fresher breeze blew in their faces and they emerged into a woodland glade very much like the one where they had met.

There was the noise of a great gate slamming, and Guyon found himself alone. The fresh air hit him in the face, as rich and sweet and choking as mandragora. All the temptations, all the hankering, all the wishing and wanting and childish longings jeered inside his brain.

What, did you think it was easy for Guyon to turn down all that money? To turn his back on being a millionaire? Could you, if it was offered to you on a golden platter? Yes, it was a trap. Of course it was a trap. Those guard-beasts would have gripped him the moment he touched a single coin… Even so! The things he could have done with that money! Yes, Mammon would have made Guyon his lifelong slave! Even so! The joys he could have bought! The palaces! The influence! The fame!

It had taken such a feat of will-power to resist, that, now the temptation was past, Guyon's brain curled up inside his head like a hibernating hedgehog. Nearby, he could hear the shushing sound of the sea. He dropped to his knees – to his hands – to his chest – and lay so deeply unconscious that anyone tripping over him would have thought him dead.

❋ ❋ ❋ ❋ ❋ ❋ ❋ ❋ ❋ ❋ ❋

CHAPTER TWO
Arthur and the Voyagers

MAROONED ON THE wrong side of the river, Palmer walked upstream, until he reached a place shallow enough to ford, feeling his way across the stony river bed with his staff. But in the maze of primeval forest, it took a long time to find Guyon. When he did, he thought he had come too late, for the knight lay motionless on his face among the leaf litter… and bending over him was a knight, his dagger drawn! Unarmed, what could Palmer do?

Archimago the Sorcerer was there, too, leaping about like a demented toad, urging, "He's the one! He's the one who shamed you, Firebrand! Kill him! He made you look a fool!"

Purple with rage, Firebrand kicked and stamped on Sir Guyon. Like all bullies, he was very daring when his foe could not hit back. He began stripping Guyon of his armour, his shield and helmet.

"Stop! Stop! Shame on you, you craven coward! Would you stoop to robbing a helpless man?" protested Palmer. But Firebrand paid no attention. Archimago gave a low cackle and capered about – until a rattle of hoof beats made him glance over his shoulder. "Draw your weapon, Firebrand!" he croaked in terror, and instantly he ran away and hid.

Into the glade rode a figure who made Firebrand leave off his pilfering and jump up. Golden armour cast a light like dappled water amid the gloom. Adorning the stranger's breastplate was a picture of the Faerie Queen.

But as Arthur passed the bush where Archimago was hiding, the golden sword at his side magically fell to the ground as if its hanger had been snicked clean through. Firebrand snatched it up and brandished it. "This yours, Outlander? Let me give it you back – point-first!"

Arthur did not seem very impressed. "I regret to inform you, sir, that my sword will do you no good. Its blade is enchanted, you see. Did you never hear the name 'Excalibur'?"

Firebrand was not listening: he knew he could beat an unarmed man.

But he had reckoned without the power of pure magic. Excalibur's golden blade would no more wound its owner than would rays from the sun or rain from the sky. Though Firebrand hacked away, the blade glanced harmlessly off. Then Palmer snatched up Sir Guyon's sword and threw it, hilt-first, into Arthur's golden grasp.

Firebrand gave a shriek of ungovernable rage, picked up a lance and flung it, striking Arthur in the side, so that he fell from his horse. The magical sheen of that golden armour flickered like a fire burning low. Unwise as ever, Firebrand turned to sneer at Palmer: "Nah nah-nah nah!"

It was all the respite Arthur needed. In a flash he was on Firebrand, tumbling him to the ground, holding a blade to his throat. "Surrender, knight! Forswear your life of crime! Swear to observe the Code of Chivalry, and I shall spare you!"

But Firebrand was burning out of control. Blazing temper had scorched all cool reason out of his head, burned up the softer side of his nature, boiled away any milk of human kindness in his veins. He died like a bonfire in a summer downpour.

Sir Guyon chose this moment to recover from his faint. He found Palmer and a knight in golden armour leaning anxiously over him. The knight's squire came cantering up, too late to enjoy the fight.

Tiny, in the distance, was the running figure of Archimago. He kept trying to snap his fingers – to summon up sprites or demons – but his hands were too slippery with sweaty fright. "Just you wait! I'll set my friend on you!" he shouted, like some angry, spoiled little child. "I'll send Maleger!"

"Who are you? Why did you risk your life to help us?" Guyon refused to go a step farther without knowing the identity of the Golden Knight. They had reached a broad river delta sprigged with the masts of sailing boats. The river led down to a shining, summer sea.

"My name is Arthur. I come from the Realm of Dreams – before that, the Realm of Albion. I came here looking to serve that most perfect of ladies, the Faerie Queen…" (He laid his hand tenderly over the portrait on his breast.) "But I keep getting side-tracked."

"Today you did a great service to Queen Gloriana without knowing it," said Guyon, and explained about his quest. "Acrasia's Bower must be destroyed, or it will snare thousands of good men! Perhaps you've seen it on your journey? Apparently it floats about – not fixed…"

"…like a ship without an anchor," breathed Palmer softly. He was looking out to sea through his pocket telescope, and pointed with his other hand: "That dark speck on the horizon… could that be it?"

Guyon turned eagerly to Arthur. "What are we waiting for? Let's find a boat and go!"

But Arthur did not move. "I'm not coming," he said. Guyon retraced his steps, disappointed. He had thought he and Arthur would make an invincible twosome. "The quest is yours, Guyon, and the glory must be yours, too," said Arthur shielding his eyes. "But Timian and I will see you safely on your way. You may not have noticed, but you have a little opposition to your quest."

And suddenly the demons were on them.

Some were repulsively ugly in war paint and with grotesque tattoos. Some kept up an ear-splitting din on bagpipes, rattles and drums. Some hurled themselves bodily, or used each other like cannonballs and battering rams. Some threw dead frogs or cowpats. In short, they assailed all five senses – offending sight and hearing and touch and smell and good taste.

Arthur and Timian received their attack as rocks receive a breaking sea. They beat off demons, while Guyon and Palmer made a dash for a sailing boat moored to the riverbank. "Keep a cool head!" said Palmer, hitching up his skirts and leaping into the boat. "When the senses fail you, let cool reason take the tiller!" (Fine time to come up with nautical platitudes!)

The demons had spotted their ploy. Without Arthur and Timian, the boat would have been overrun in no time – holed or capsized, or set alight by burning arrows. Palmer pushed off from shore, using his staff.

Arthur was head-and-shoulders taller than the demons, but they were numberless as swarming ants – the Stinkers, the Blinders, the Sickeners, the Rowdies, the Touchers. And when at last he scattered them, with sword, mace and bare hands, he found he had only cleared the path for their leader: a creature more hideous than all the rest. It was Archimago's friend.

It was Maleger.

Maleger was a carcass of a man, dressed all in canvas except for his helmet, which was made from a skull. He came mounted on a tiger with two hags for his outriders. All three looked like a frail jumble of bones, but looks can be misleading. For one thing, they had too little flesh to feel pain, and their bony heads rattled with the cunning of several lifetimes.

Looking back from the stern of his boat, Guyon saw Arthur lose his footing and the haggard outriders wheel down on him from either flank, holding him down, pinning him to the ground. Back came Maleger, speedy on his soft-pawed tiger, sword drawn, bony mouth agape…

"Pull for the shore! Stop! I must go back and help him!" cried Guyon.

But Palmer would not allow it. "You have your quest. Arthur has his."

Then in rushed Timian, and jabbed the hags in their bony bottoms, making them let go their grip on Arthur. Arthur parried Maleger's death blow and felled the death's-head warrior to the ground. It was blow enough to kill most men, but Maleger only laughed, picked up a fistful of dirt and crammed it into his mouth as though it were food.

"Don't you know, pretty knight, that the Earth gave birth to me?" he jeered. "The Earth is my mother! She feeds me!" And when he saw Arthur throw aside his golden sword, Maleger laughed out loud, thinking he had broken the knight's nerve.

But Arthur had discarded his sword only so as to free his hands. He folded Maleger in his arms – lifted his feet off the ground – held him suspended in mid-air – and crushed the wind out of his lungs and the beat out of his heart… before throwing him in the river.

"Come, Timian!" cried Arthur, pulling his squire from under a pile of demons. "Onward to Cleopolis!"

For three days Sir Guyon and Palmer sailed across the sea.

Once they sighted mermaids sitting on a reef, combing their long green hair, crooning songs at the voyagers. "Put your hands over your ears," said Palmer, tight-lipped, arms folded, deaf to the unsettling music.

"They seem to like us," said Guyon.

"Like us?" said Palmer. "They love us. But only like roast parsnips or a side of beef. They want to get you ashore and eat you."

When their charms failed, the mermaids went back to sucking and

nibbling on the whitening bones that lay mounded up around them like the twigs of a gigantic nest.

Guyon and Palmer rowed… and found themselves in among a flotilla of little islands, each one prettier than the last. Could one of these be Acrasia's floating island? They were tiny patches of paradise – or so it seemed to Guyon. "Let's moor up… rest… all that rowing… exhausted!"

Palmer pursed his lips in that way Guyon had come to know and dread.

"Don't tell me. They were built by alien locusts."

"You would never want to leave. Believe me: comfort can be as treacherous as quicksand," said Palmer. Guyon thought back to the ferrywoman and rowed on.

But there was nothing either comfortable or tempting about what came next over the side of the boat: a suckered tentacle – feeling, reaching, grasping, embracing… "Palmer!"

Heads rose out of the sea around them – monstrous heads grisly with fangs, tusks, horns and spines. They drew back rubbery lips and groaned, pitching in the water, lunging at the little boat, all but swamping it. A hydra with seven heads, a knot of water snakes, a sea elephant with barnacled tusks wallowed and thrashed about: a marine stampede. Furry flukes slapped the water into a frenzy. Stinging tendrils planted toxic kisses on the underside of the boat. Guyon sat frozen with terror. "Sit down, Palmer! You'll turn us over! Sit down!"

But Palmer was standing up in the prow, reaching out his staff. Like a warrior with a quarterstaff, he whacked the water: once, twice, three times.

The monsters gave a gargling roar and sank out of sight, leaving behind only the stench of rotting fish. Even the sucker marks on the back of Guyon's hand faded away.

"Illusions," said Palmer. "Acrasia must have conjured them to keep away unwelcome visitors. It's a good sign. It means we are nearing the Bower."

Guyon said nothing. He was watching the fog descend.

It came down as thick as wool, but clammy and damp. The sun was extinguished and a kind of grey midnight settled on the boat. They heard the flutter of wings: bats and owls and vultures that circled and screeched and roosted on the cross-tree of the mast. Their fanning wings would have stood Guyon's hair on end if it were not already upright with fear.

"Just illusions, right?" said Guyon.

"No. They are real enough," said Palmer. "They sense calamity coming."

"I hope you mean calamity for Acrasia."

"How would I know? I'm not a fortune teller," said Palmer testily.

The fog cleared. The sun returned as bright as ever. It shone on an ocean as smooth as glass – and on an island of incomparable loveliness.

Nothing had prepared Sir Guyon for what he saw. Think of the loveliest, happiest, most delectable place you have ever been; alongside the Bower of Bliss, it would be a wet slag-heap. Acrasia had constructed the land at the end of everyone's rainbow.

❄ ❄ ❄ ❄ ❄ ❄ ❄ ❄ ❄ ❄ ❄

CHAPTER THREE
The Bower of Bliss

BUT THE BOWER did not welcome uninvited visitors. Acrasia kept guard dogs – and panthers, boar, jackals, bulls and apes. At the sight of Guyon and Palmer dragging their boat up the powdery blond beach, this menagerie came bounding, roaring and snarling, baring needle-sharp teeth.

Once, twice, three times Palmer swung his staff before Guyon's sword was even out of its scabbard. The beasts faltered, stopped short, turned tail and ran, whining and gibbering, back in among the trees.

"I think you might have mentioned that magic staff of yours before," said Guyon.

"Why? It might have made you over-confident," said Palmer. "That would never do. Besides, my staff does not make us invincible. I hope you remembered the net."

It was a net of fine wire mesh. Guyon just hoped he would know what to do with it when the time came. They pressed inland – into the welcome shade of the trees: the sun was high in the sky and the day was hot. They had to skirt an exquisite filigree fence until they found the way in.

The gatekeeper, luckily, was far more welcoming than the wild beasts had been. In fact he thrust a large china bowl of cool wine into Guyon's hands. The aromatic liquor was seeded with bubbles. It slopped against his fingertips, delicious, refreshing...

But Guyon had learnt a thing or two on his travels. He glanced at Palmer whose eyes were narrowed with caution. Then he smashed the bowl on the ground where it broke. Wine is all very well, but it has been the undoing of many a good man and woman.

"What d'you do that for? Hooligan!" complained the gatekeeper, but Guyon and Palmer shouldered him aside and entered Acrasia's garden. Instantly they could hear the noise of laughter, the giggling of fountains, singing birds. Umbelliferous flowers drooped their heavy perfumed heads over the upturned faces of roses and peonies, while lilies trumpeted their beauty into the shifting dapple of leaf-shade. Little silver brooks and every colour of tiny flowerhead embellished the grass beneath their feet. A fountain as tall as the mast of a ship rose from the heart of a lake surrounded by silvery weeping willows. Fruit dangled within easy reach, and no pathway was straight, but rambled in and out of flowery nooks past views of unimaginable perfection receding into the smoke-blue of the distance. Like cream in a dairy, white fair-weather clouds were piled in the great blue bowl of the sky.

"Surely nowhere so beautiful could be a work of evil?" said Guyon.

"It depends why it was put here," said Palmer, blinkering his eyes, refusing to look. Guyon, though, drank his fill. He gazed and stared until his head reeled – at the cherry blossom, the waterfalls, the scarlet dogwoods and espaliered peaches.

So where had Guyon got the impression that this island was a witch's lair? From Palmer. What if Palmer was just born joyless: a killjoy – the sort of man who begrudges happiness and sneers at beauty because he has neither?

Beauty is good, he decided. Can you have too much of a good thing?

"Are you weakening, Guyon?" asked Palmer.

The perfumes in the air grew stronger with every step they took. Then there were voices:

> *"Gather the roses while you may:*
> *The time is flying!*
> *Gather the roses while you may:*
> *We all are dying!"*

"Tread softly," said Palmer. "We are very close now. We must take Acrasia by surprise or she will slip through our grasp."

And there it was – the Bower of Bliss that Guyon had come so far to destroy. Now he understood the temptation that had captivated so many knights. How could any man have stumbled on to this and not been tempted?

On a bed of crimson rose petals, a young knight lay asleep in a woman's lap. His armour hung from a nearby tree – tin to scare the crows away. The woman was stroking his hair, singing her magical song softly into his ear, drowning him in magical bliss.

"What did you expect?" breathed Palmer. "A pointed black hat and a cauldron?"

At the mere sight of her, jealousy and desire and fiery passion and icy misery besieged Guyon. With so lovely a woman, love-at-first-sight was entirely possible. In a moment she would look up and see him and then... and then... he would be powerless to resist...

"Now!" said Palmer.

Guyon shut his eyes, his ears, his nose, his lips against his body's yearnings. He was a house locking its doors and windows against the assailants outside. Before he could think better of it, he unrolled and threw the steel net. It settled over Acrasia and the knight like fishing net over two pink salmon. They cried out, struggled and cursed, bloodying their fingers on the wire. But the more they struggled the more entangled they became.

Meanwhile, Palmer and Guyon set about their task of destruction. They took axes to the trees, sword and stick to the flowers and fruit. Their boots crushed the rose petals black. What they could not hack down they set alight, raising a great pall of dirty, evil-smelling smoke that blacked out the creamy clouds.

Then Acrasia's magic crumbled and peeled like painted plaster, for it had no depth. Reality rolled ashore in its place: dreary rain, a chill, dank wind, canker and wilt and disease.

The young knight inside the net blinked and writhed and recovered his memory, begging now to be separated from this woman who had taken him captive. They prised him loose, like a crab from a crab-pot. Acrasia herself pleaded, bargained and wheedled. But Guyon was stoniest rock. Guyon was immune. Guyon had achieved his quest. He had kept his head. He had kept to the Golden Mean.

The birds flew away; the fountains and lakes were choked with ash; the fruit lay pulped on the ground. The animals in blind panic herded this way and that, as trees went up in plumes of flame or stood reduced to blackened leafless skeletons.

"What are you?" Acrasia railed at them from inside the net. "What kind of men destroy beauty and peace and music and happiness? What kind of vandal burns flowers and chops down paradise?"

Guyon pursed his mouth tight. He wanted to blinker his eyes with his hands. He wanted her to be quiet.

But Palmer had an answer ready for Acrasia. "Only God can build Paradise, witch. Your bower was a fake, a counterfeit, a honey-trap. It was a painted paradise made with mischief in mind!" And he began dragging the net down to the sea, filling the witch's hair with sand.

They were loading it into the boat when, out of the burning woods came the wild animals, even more furious than before.

"So do we kill the animals now?" Guyon asked, drawing his sword.

"Animals?" said Palmer, his staff outstretched, "Hold your hand, knight. These creatures were once like you and I. Don't you remember? Once Acrasia tires of toying with a man, she turns him into a wild beast — the one closest to him in nature. It's her idea of a joke."

One by one, he touched each beast with his magic staff.

One by one they moulted their fur, shed antlers and tusks, lost their stripes or scales. Soon a huddle of naked men cowered on the ground, weeping with misery, sobbing with relief. "Thank you! Oh thank you!" they said, savouring the taste of words in their mouths once more.

Only one resented being rescued.

"What d'you wanna change Grille back for?" groaned a gross, lardy man with small, close-set eyes and a mouthful of rotten peaches. "Grille liked being a pig! Nobody made Grille work. Nobody made Grille get up when the mud was cool, or stop eating while there was still food to be had!" He picked up bruised pomegranate and crammed it into his mouth, cursing as he munched and slobbered. "Interfering do-gooders! Meddling wretches! Grille was better off as a pig. Nobody messes with pigs."

Palmer nudged the man's shoulder with his magic staff… and Grille was a pig once more, rootling and snuffling through the fallen fruit, eating and wallowing and snorting, waddling through the smoking ruins of the Bower.

Some men make better animals than people.

"So. You finally came back to us, Sir Guyon," said the Faerie Queen, legs curled up among the curly cascade of her golden hair. The fabric of her gown was woven from cobwebs on a sunny morning: cobwebs and magic.

"Tell us what you learned during your quest."

Guyon stared into the middle-distance, seeking the right words. "I learned to steer a course between too little and too much. A middle way. A moderate way. Not too hot, not too cold. Not rash nor lazy. I learned not to be a slave to my senses but to keep a cool head. Everything in moderation and nothing to excess."

The Faerie Queen regarded him, her head on one side, studying this paragon of serenity and self-control. Even his hair seemed less red. "The Golden Mean's a tightrope, I always think: so easy to fall off… Of course, you would never have reached the Bower without this Arthur you speak of."

"Absolutely!" Guyon admitted.

"How rash he must be! How extraordinary! How very, very… Where was I? Yes, yes. Congratulations, my Knight of the Golden Mean, on saving the world from Acrasia! Not that your work is done. The world is full of Passion. Agonies and Ecstasies. Rapture. Despair. Please be patient with those of u— with those people who cannot match your temperate nature."

If you ask me, I think I liked Guyon's hair when it was redder, but what do I know?

Book Three
~
Cambell All But
Rides Down Friendship

Chapter One
Fair Canacee

Sir Cambell is one of the Queen's favourites. She gave him a magic ring that heals any kind of wound. She could give them to all her knights, but I suppose she prefers not to meddle overmuch with Fate.

Last year at the Festival, Cambell set himself his own personal quest, and he did not have to travel far from Cleopolis to fulfil it. His little sister's beauty was causing chaos and mayhem within seven shires of Faerie. Canacee was so lovely that she no sooner came of age than knights were queuing at the gate asking to marry her. It could not go on – the quarrels, the preening, the swooning, the swaggering… So Cambell determined to find her a fit husband – the very best.

He said that whoever could fight him and win could have Canacee's hand. This was not quite as reckless as it sounds, because, as everyone knows, Cambell has this magic ring. It makes him almost invincible.

Suddenly the queues at the gate drifted away. The serenades under Canacee's window fell silent. Poems stopped arriving by every messenger. How was anyone going to beat a knight with a magic ring?

Only three were prepared to try. And they were all brothers.

Now you might think that three boys born on the same day would have had to share their mother's love three ways. Not these. When their mother, Agape gave birth to triplets she simply loved each boy three times as much. Her every thought centred on Priamond, Diamond and Triamond and on making them happy. And though she had one lovely daughter already – and friends – and her studies of the magic arts to occupy her – it seemed to Agape that happiness itself depended on her three boys.

What if anything should happen to them? What if any harm should come to them? Worry (always the itchy lining of motherhood) began to chafe at her, disturbing her nights, spoiling her days. The boys were brave like their father – rash and reckless like their father. Surely they would no sooner be grown than they would put themselves in terrible dangers, performing feats of bravery!

So Agape went to visit The Fates – those three gaunt hags who spin out our Destinies like a hank of knitting wool. They looked her over with unblinking

eyes set in expressionless faces, one spinning her distaff, one measuring out the spun thread, one cutting it through with a great pair of shears: A birth... A span of life... A death...

"I have come about my sons," said Agape. "Priamond. Diamond. Triamond. I must know... Will they live long? I won't lose them, will I? I couldn't bear it if..."

Snip, snip went the ancient hag with the silver shears. She held up two short wisps of wool: barely more than snippets.

"A man's fate cannot be changed, Agape. Go home."

But Agape did not go. She wept and screamed and pleaded, and would not stop until she had wrung two tiny words of comfort from the hags. Pity from the pitiless.

If Priamond died first, his life force would pass into Diamond.

If Diamond died, then the two lives within him would pass into Triamond.

It wasn't much, but it was better than nothing in a cruel world.

Agape guarded her boys as a lioness guards her cubs. She ringed them round with all the magic at her disposal. Best of all, she taught them,

Be to each other always true;

Love one another, as I have loved you.

So they never once quarrelled or brawled or even disagreed. In fact, they were in perfect accord over everything. Agape really thought her love had reshaped their Destiny... until love of a different kind came along.

One sight of Canacee and all three brothers felt the same pang. Her brother was no deterrent, ring or no ring. They would fight Cambell, come what may, and one of them would win the lovely Canacee.

Up went the tourney lists, the pavilions, the banners. On went the saddlecloths, the armour, and the gauntlets. There in the stands sat six judges; there on a high platform sat Canacee, praying for Fate to send her a worthy husband, praying still harder that no harm come to her dear brother.

Out rode Cambell, to the blare of trumpets, to meet the challenge of Priamond.

Lance against lance they rode, jarring each other's shields. They were equally matched, though an unlucky lance-point glanced off Cambell's shield and ran clean through his shoulder. Not a drop of blood ran from the wound (though the pain was no less for all that). Cambell dropped his shield and swayed in the saddle, but retaliated, driving his lance in under Priamond's shield and into his thigh where it broke off.

Priamond gave a roar of pain and rage. "I've only let you live this long for your sister's sake! Prepare to die!" And he flung his lance at Cambell's head, striking it so hard that Cambell was flung backwards in the saddle. The spectators screamed. But the lance had broken off and, wound or no wound, Cambell was pulling the stumpy point from his helmet's visor and throwing it back at Priamond's face. It struck him in the throat. His soul spilled out, like bees from a holed hive... and flew directly to Diamond his brother.

So, instead of horror and sorrow at the loss of his beloved brother, Diamond felt only fiery rage and a surge of energy pumping through his heart. Swamped with the fever of battle, unlooping his axe from his saddle, he came riding at Cambell as though at the devil himself.

Diamond was strong; he was adept. He hammered Cambell's shield out of shape and cut him about the shoulders and legs. The only art he lacked was patience, and finally, unable to bear the to and fro, up and down, hand-to-hand combat, he took his axe by its haft and threw it at Cambell.

If it had struck home, even the magic ring would not have saved him, but Cambell ducked and, as he ducked, swung his axe...

For a moment, Diamond did not fall. The spectators sat stock still, too, hands over their mouths, eyes wide. Then twin souls, like two birds flying from the same tree, darted from the throat of Diamond... and nested beneath the breastplate of Triamond.

Triamond. His grief pained him like an axe wound, but his strength and

72

his lust for life were suddenly three times as great. That Cambell could still even crawl on hands and knees defied belief, seeing how gashed and slashed and battered his two adversaries had left him. And yet the magic of Gloriana's ring was still at work. Like a snake that sheds its skin and recovers the sheen and colours of its youth, so Cambell recovered his strength. Pain encased him, but his blood still coursed and his sinews held.

Canacee could barely see for the tears that streamed from her eyes. What happy outcome could there be to this slaughter? Either her brother would die, or the only man left who loved her enough to dare all.

The fighting was hand-to-hand now, a brawl lacking all style and grace, a wrestling match amid the wounded horses, blood, fallen weapons and broken armour. The judges were on their feet; the spectators had begun to moan and groan and ask how anything could be solved this way.

Cambell and Triamond were only dimly aware of their surroundings, slugging and slamming away at one another with fist and foot and head. But somehow they became aware of a change in the noise. Now they were hearing screams, gasps and running feet. They looked round and saw that some of the crowd were struggling to get down from the stands. Someone or something had entered the field of combat and was bearing down on the combatants.

The chariot was gold, and not only the chariot, but the creatures pulling it — two snarling, rampant lions. It seemed for a moment that an angel chariot had been sent to fetch home the dead to Heaven. The woman around

whose small waist the chariot reins were tied had all the brightness and beauty of an angel. In one hand she held a wand wound with two serpents; in the other a goblet filled to the slopping brim with purple liquor. Triamond's eyes were on the lions — their manes ablaze with evening light, their jaws agape. But Cambell was looking at the rider. All noise was muffled, all time slowed, all thoughts snowbound by the sight of that angel-charioteer.

She drove clear between them, the chariot wheels brushing the welts of their boots. The faces of antique kings decorating the chariot's golden sides passed so close that Cambell and Triamond brushed noses with Xerxes and Xenophon. The gauntlets dropped from their dangling hands and lay like dead pheasants at their feet.

"Cambina!" breathed Triamond.

She stepped down, her face awash with tears, and lay down between them on the ground. "Stop this fight! End this now! You have both proved whatever it is you meant to prove. Marriages don't grow by being watered with blood! Make an end, here and now, for the sake of the ladies who love you!"

"You know this lady?" said Cambell to his opponent.

"She's my sister," said Triamond blushing a little. "Don't mind her. You know what sisters are like." And so saying, he stepped across the woman stretched out on the ground and put up his bare fists, ready to fight on.

"Drink, at least!" cried Cambina, rising to her feet, offering them the cup of cool, delicious liquor. "You must be hot! And your throats are full of dust. Drink!"

So they took the cup, and first Cambell, then Triamond drank as only thirsty men can. As they drank, Cambina rapped them softly with her magic, healing wand.

While Priamond and Diamond and Triamond had mewled and gurgled and burped their way through babyhood, their sister Cambina had studied. While their faerie mother had wept in the deep dark caves of the Fates, her young daughter Cambina had studied her mother's books of magic, read the ancient classics, roamed the fields in search of herbs and stirred concoctions with her mother's magic wand.

And somehow, she had brewed nepenthe. Nepenthe: brew of the gods — made to be drunk in Heaven, whenever grief or anger or regret gnawed too hard on their immortal hearts. It has the power to wash away the rage of a volcano, the salty sorrow of a sea. Just as the tide scours out a tangle of footprints on the sand, so nepenthe washes clean the memory and leaves a smooth nothing behind.

Suddenly, neither Cambell nor Triamond could remember why they were there, bruised and bleeding amid a wilderness of carnage. They could not remember why they had been fighting. All they remembered was a deep and dogged friendship between them that stretched back to who-knows when. They were the best of friends; they had always been friends. The man was not born who could come between Triamond and Cambell!

Fortunately Cambell did remember Cambina, and that he had fallen in love with her at first sight.

"Can I marry your sister?" said Cambell, watching Cambina unharness the lions.

"By all means!" exclaimed Triamond. "We can have a double wedding!"

Canacee found her own way down from the high platform on which she had sat like a sports trophy. She was filled with such tenderness, such fond feelings, such loving gratitude that she ran and flung her arms around her dearest friend in the world: Cambina.

And the two sat happily together on the ground, bemoaning the foolishness of men, the folly of battle and the mess that lions leave behind. Meanwhile, the men shared the last of the nepenthe and congratulated each other on what splendid wives they had found themselves.

Queen Gloriana dubbed Cambell and Triamond jointly her 'Knights of Friendship', for as she says, how could the virtue possibly be represented by a single man?

BOOK FOUR
~
BRITOMART RIDES OUT IN
HOPE OF PURE LOVE

CHAPTER ONE
Of Knights and Knighties

❖ BRITOMART'S QUEST DID not start at Cleopolis. Indeed, Britomart did not start out as a knight. She was skilled in the use of weapons and could ride as well as anyone, but that came of having brothers. In fact, Britomart did not start out as Britomart – her name was Brita – and she would have been perfectly content to live at home… until the day she saw the mirror.

It was not really a mirror at all but a sort of globule of glass, smoky at its heart. Once it had belonged to Merlin the Magician, but he had given it to Brita's father, and Brita came across it one day, by chance, in a loft. She looked into its misshapen centre and, in the heart of the glass, saw… nothing – just a cloudy spiral distorting her reflection. Then the smoke took on colours – purple and aquamarine – and there was the glitter of water, the bright twinkle of fish.

Britomart sat down, so as to look more closely. She saw the flash of armour, the clash of spear on shield. She gasped at the sight of a wall of fire and then a bleeding, still-beating heart cupped in the palm of a man's hand. A man

81

with elephant ears and the tusks of a boar leered out at her from the maelstrom, making her snatch her face away. Other images swept by like rubbish in a swollen river. Then the chaos within the glass cleared and she saw a young man's face.

The image laid itself like a hand on her brain.

In an instant, the mirror was a glassblower's reject once more: a lump of opaque silica; a blind eye.

But that night at supper, Brita had no appetite. She would not eat a mouthful. Her old nurse, Glauce (who was like a mother to Brita) felt her forehead and took her pulse. "Are you ill, child?"

Brita only shook her head and said she was not a child.

Within a week she had begun to faint, to run a fever, to stare out of windows, to neglect her books. She grew pale and thin.

"Are you ill, child?" asked her father.

"Not ill," said Brita.

Finally, Glauce cornered her in the rose bower. "Who is he, then? Own up. I know lovesickness when I see it!"

Brita burst into tears. "That's just it! I don't know who he is! I saw him in Father's magic mirror!"

"Ah!"

"So there's nothing to be done, is there? If that mirror shows the future, then I shall meet him one day. He's my Fate. I just have to wait! Only…"

"Hmmm. Fate can drag its feet sometimes," said Glauce understandingly.

"What else can I do? I don't know where to find him! He's a knight – an elfin knight; that much I know. And so beautiful! Oh Glauce! He has the best face a man ever wore! But there's nothing to be done!"

"You could always go and look for him," said Glauce.

Brita stared at her. A woman? Go travelling alone, God knew where?

"Mmmmm," said Glauce. "I was thinking you might disguise yourself. As a knight… Or should that be a knightie?"

So Brita put on her brother's armour, hid her long golden hair under a metal helmet and became Britomart. For extra safety she took with her a magic lance – another treasure of her father's. Even so, watching her go, Glauce wrung her hands and wondered if hers had been such a good idea.

As Britomart rode towards Faerie Land, she half expected, at every bend in the road, to meet her knight – the face in the mirror. He would look at her (she thought) and their hearts would cleave together like twin magnets.

But the first group of knights she saw were anything but attractive. They were bullies attacking a man – six against one – and they had him trapped against the base of a high castle wall. Suppose the man in difficulty was her true love! Suppose that red-cross shield held up to fend off blows concealed the sweetest face in the world!

Britomart scattered the attackers like a cat scaring birds. The magic tip of her lance frightened them into a yelping run.

"Thank you, sir knight!" said Sir George stumbling to his feet, gasping for breath. "I am indebted to you! Those rogues wanted me to forswear my Lady Una in favour of one of theirs!"

"Forswear your lady?" gasped Britomart. "But that's against all the Laws of Chivalry!" (Britomart would rather have died than forswear her knight-in-the-mirror.)

"That's what I told them," said Sir George looking around for his horse. "Should I know you, sir?"

Britomart was staring at him, examining by turns his ears, his eyes, his hair. Rain plinked on their dusty armourplate. "No. I'm afraid I've never seen you before…" she sighed. "Should we ask at this castle, do you think, for shelter and a place to sleep?"

"Good idea."

The castle was pretty, with flowers in the dry moat and garlands round the towers. Its owner too was pretty, though a little wild around the eyes and neckline. "Welcome to Castle Joyous! My doors are always open to young men of your… ooooff, calibre." The Lady Loosie looked Britomart over, like a horse looking at an apple and nodded her mane of hair appreciatively.

There was a lot of Lady Loosie's hair. It hung down in ringlets among the lacings of her dress, the ribbons of her choker.

All evening her feet bumped Britomart's under the table, and she laughed delightedly at every remark Britomart passed. Britomart could not look up without catching a wink or the playful wiggle of flirty fingers. Britomart had the terrible sinking feeling that, in her disguise, she had accidentally won the heart of Lady Loosie.

As soon as she was able, she asked to go to bed and was shown to a very comfortable room, which (to her great relief) she did not have to share with Sir George. She was able to shed all her armour and climb into bed wearing only her shift.

But no sooner had she drifted off to sleep than a noise woke her and she felt the bedclothes shifting. A head settled into the pillow alongside hers. "Such a very... pretty knight," crooned a lady's voice. "Embrace me, sir, do!"

"Woah!" cried Britomart sitting bolt upright.

"What?" The moon was hidden. The bed seemed to be full of hands and hair and misunderstandings. Brita gave a scream. So did Loosie. "Who...?"

Britomart rolled out of bed and, in groping around for her boots, knocked over the fire irons. Lady Loosie reached out and inadvertently grabbed a handful of hair. "Huh?"

"Ow!" Britomart grabbed up her armour like so many dinner plates and hopped off down the passage, one boot on and one boot off.

Roused by raised voices, Sir George stumbled from his room, sword in hand. "Who goes there?"

Britomart shut her eyes so as not to see Sir George in his short shirt and so collided with a suit of armour on the landing, sending it clattering down the stairs. Bewildered, Sir George followed the slap of bare feet and the sound of a magic lance rapping its clackety way down the stairs while, behind him, the landing echoed to female howling. Blindly the two visitors fumbled their way across the Great Hall, Sir George thinking he was chasing an intruder, Britomart thinking she was still being pursued by the amorous lady of the house.

Only on the drawbridge, as the moon came out from behind a cloud, did everything become plain.

"What the—?" said Sir George.

"Don't look!" said Brita as, buckle by buckle, she became Britomart again. Only her moonlight hair, falling like a waterfall over her steel epaulettes, gave the game away. They stared at each other, she wide-eyed with maidenly fright, he trying to fit his boots through the legs of his trousers.

Then he collected himself and bowed deeply. "My mistake, comrade," he said gallantly.

"I think the Lady Loosie mistook me…" whispered Britomart, pointing up at the castle.

"I don't blame her for that," said Sir George, "only for treating Love as if it were nothing more than a game. We knights know it to be the highest and noblest quest of a pure heart!"

"Oh yes!" exclaimed Britomart, clasping her hands. "The noblest quest of a pure heart!" And finding George a man after her own heart, she told him about the face in the mirror, about her quest to find the owner of the face.

"That will be Artegall," said Sir George as she described the heraldry she had seen in the glass.

"You know him?!"

"Everyone at Cleopolis knows Artegall... though I don't know just where he is at present: sometimes he likes to ride off and get grubby — right wrongs — win tournaments, that sort of thing."

"And is he... does he... he isn't... would you say... is he... a good knight?" she asked, terrified that the mirror had bamboozled her.

"Artegall? The best! Absolutely."

Still Britomart trembled. "And single?"

"That too," said George, hiding his smile with a yawn.

CHAPTER TWO
Florimell and the Merman

THEY PARTED COMPANY, Britomart and Sir George, and what Britomart did next set in train another adventure altogether.

She came to the seashore and there, strewn along the beach like so much seaweed was the most extraordinary array of treasure she had ever seen. There were pearls plentiful as frogspawn, silver plates, mother-of-pearl knives, golden chains-of-office, casks of Spanish wine. These valuables lay higgledy-piggledy among pretty sea-dross — green-lipped oysters, fish scales, corals, bells and figureheads from wrecked ships. Like a traveller in an eastern bazaar she let her horse pick its way through.

"You must hold your life cheap, knight, that you trespass on my property and pilfer my belongings!"

From behind a rock stepped a young man, exceedingly handsome if a little green in the face. In fact, on closer inspection he was green all over, like a statue cast in copper that the weather has stained with verdigris. Even his sword was blue-green.

"I didn't know the beach was yours, sir," said Britomart. "And I don't pilfer."

"I know you dry-land pirates! You help yourself to whatever you fancy. Thieves and looters!" And he came at her, wielding his blue-green sword, so that she was obliged to put up her shield. Tugging her lance from its leather socket, she lowered its magic-tipped point and, in his blind fury, the young man ran directly on to it.

"Oh! I'm sorry! Let me help you!" she cried as he clutched his shoulder. But his face only contorted with anger and bafflement: "Either kill me or get off my beach!"

Britomart withdrew. She had no argument with this sea-coloured boy and no desire for his riches. Looking back, she saw he had sunk to his knees among the treasure chests and wine-kegs and might well be going to die. But she dared not go back for fear he wasted his last strength trying to fight her. Britomart bit her lip and roused her horse to a gallop. With luck, the boy had a sweetheart nearby who would tend to his injuries.

Marinell had no sweetheart, nor ever would have. Ever since the Prophecy, his mother Cymo had helped him to avoid women. His father, King of the Sea, had showered him with the sea's wealth, trying to compensate the boy for going without female company. For the Prophecy had said he would be laid low by a beautiful, virgin maiden.

Each day he told himself: better alive and alone, than in love and dead.

Now Marinell lay on the beach, his life-blood welling out of him into the sand, and wondered what cruel mistake had brought him to this. Why had he made do with tawdry, trashy treasure only to be killed — and not by a maiden at all, but by some passing knight!

87

An oceanic blackness larger than the incoming tide washed over him and he sank into sandy oblivion.

The waves began to break the news, the seagulls to cry. The doors in deep ocean began to slam and the rumour was carried far and wide by the currents. Any shell pressed to the ear that day would have whispered the same words: *Prince Marinell lies dead.*

The news reached Princess Florimell in her coastline castle. She would sooner have heard that the sea had turned to blood, that the sky had smashed like a window, that the moon had been stolen. All her life she had loved Marinell secretly and from afar. Bad enough that he had sworn never to marry! Must she now go on living, knowing he was dead?

Something inside Florimell broke like a magic mirror, and she ran out-of-doors half mad with grief. Servants and courtiers ran after her, but Florimell outstripped them. She was running as if from wolves – as if to outrun the news, outrun her misery, outrun her life…

Marinell's mother Cymo, hearing the selfsame news, leapt to her sea-chariot and urged her dolphins over the pitching sea. Jumping down into the surf, she dragged her sodden skirts through the shallows and ran to his side. "Son! My son!" The waves were lifting his head, swilling his hair over his face, bumping his skull on the grumbling pebbles.

But Marinell was not dead.

Finding the flicker of a pulse, the sea nymph lifted her son and laid him in her chariot. The dolphins curbed their boisterous leaping, the sea curbed its tossing, the wind held its breath and the sea-chariot glided as far as the horizon, before diving to the bottom of the sea…

Florimell ran until she had no more strength to run. Marinell dead? Then why was she still living? She felt invisible – as if her tears had washed her as transparent as glass. But she was not.

Her headlong dash caught the eye of a forester – a lewd, lazy man, but one ready to put on a canter to catch a pretty little female. When Florimell heard his big boots crushing the leaves behind her, she glanced round and let out a scream. She could see that her troubles had only just begun.

There was someone nearby who could have helped, but in her blind panic she ran right past him. Timian, Arthur's squire, saw at a glance what was happening and set off to the rescue. By the time the forester reached a stream and started across it, Timian was close on his heels, shouting in the deepest, most manly voice he could muster: "Stand and fight, you cur!"

Unfortunately, this particular cur came from a large litter. On the other side of the stream, two of his brothers emerged from the trees, dragging cudgels. Timian skidded to a halt – looked around for help, but found none. The three thugs surrounded him, knocked his puny dagger out of his hand, then laid about him with their boots and clubs, laughing, staining the pure stream water with his blood. By the time they left him, he was no more than meat-bones for the wolves and wild boar to pick clean.

As for Florimell, she outran everyone – friend and foe – and found herself at the door of a little cottage. An old peasant – a tiny crab apple of a woman – welcomed her with a rosy smile. Not until Florimell was indoors did she meet the woman's son – a great lummocking mountain of sweating acne, called Block. Sometimes, in a bright light, Block was so clever he could remember all the way back to breakfast time.

All his lardy life Block had wanted a wife like Florimell. Florimell politely explained that her heart was already given, and broke down in tears, thinking of Marinell lying dead on the shore. The old woman patted her hand consolingly – then set about changing her mind. She picked some herbs, mixed some potions…

She was, after all, a witch.

❋   ❋   ❋   ❋   ❋   ❋   ❋   ❋   ❋   ❋   ❋

CHAPTER THREE
Under the Sea

CYMO THE SEA nymph, driving her chariot over the sobbing sea, looked down at her wounded son and wept. She regretted now her lifelong advice to Marinell never to love, never to marry. Better to have crammed his days with tenderness and love than to have wasted his life in a barren, gem-studded desert. The Prophecy had been wrong! A knight and not a 'virgin-maid' had inflicted this terrible wound!

Between the foam-topped waves shone the spires and minarets of Neptune's palace. Phosphorescent bubbles broke from each gill-slit window, each cuttle-shell chimney, each baleen skylight. Down the steep spiral of a whirlpool Cymo plunged to her bower – an opalescent space like a nimbus cloud, enclosed by hollow waves. Here she laid Marinell on a couch while she sent the dolphins to fetch the Sea Healer. "Hurry!" she called after them. "My boy's life is ebbing away!"

Timian the page opened his eyes and thought he was in heaven. Leaning over him, her long hair brushing his face, was a woman too lovely to be mortal flesh and blood. She was dressed as a hunter, a golden bow across her back, a quiver on her hip.

Something inside young Timian yearned towards her like the arrow of a compass yearning for North. There was a pungent smell of herbs and wild flowers – the medicines of the forest – with which she had bathed and dressed his wounds. The sun stood behind her head, so that sunlight gilded her outline.

She called herself Belphoebe.

Timian loved her in an instant. In the next instant he remembered the foresters and their great clubs of wood – "You must be careful, lady! These wood are dangerous!" – but fell back, too weary to rise and defend his lady.

"Peace, boy. Your courage does you credit. But you must let me heal you, and healing begins with rest."

So began a kind of waking dream, when Timian ceased to serve Arthur and served Belphoebe the wood nymph instead. He did not look to be loved in return. He did not ask for kisses. He did not expect kindness or caresses. All he asked was to worship the perfect Belphoebe.

And she let him.

As soon as Florimell saw the look in Block's eyes, she threw down her cup undrunk and darted between mother and son and out of the door. The witch shrieked, "Catch her, Block!" Florimell's belt caught on a nail, but she was moving so fast that it simply snapped clean through and was left dangling from the latch.

Through the woods she went, on feet still sore from the previous chase. Here, there was snow on the ground, which hid sharp stones without cushioning them, froze her feet without dulling them to pain. She knew the odious Block would not catch her easily: he was about as nimble as a whelk.

But the witch did not send her son in pursuit. She sent her pet instead. "Don't fret, son. Petal will soon fetch her back," she said cheerily, and opened the door of the bread oven. Like the pellet from an owl's throat, a creature shot out, teeth bared, perpetually hungry, everlastingly eager to eat. "Fetch, Petal! Good Petal, fetch!"

One sniff of the broken belt and it was away through the door, paws threading between the girl's footprints in the snow, jaw drooling. Florimell heard it behind her and cried out with horror. She burst from the woods and on to a beach. Sand swallowed her feet. At every step she stumbled and fell and picked herself up again, sandy from head to foot. Seeing a boat drawn up above the rime of weed, she threw herself against its stern and heaved it into the surf. It banged and bullied her, threatening to push her under or capsize on top of her.

The witch's hyena came barking over the dunes, holding the belt in its mouth, rolling its yellow eyes. Florimell dragged herself over the gunwale and slithered head first into several inches of dirty water. The boat drifted out to sea in sickening dips, turning round and round in the wind, leaving the shore far behind.

Thwarted, Petal snarled and yapped in the shallows while the sea-spray caked its spotted fur in salt. Turning inshore again, it was confronted by an elfin knight. But being without brain or soul, it saw nothing to fear… until it lay dead across the boots of Sir Scudamore, knight of Cleopolis.

Scudamore was on his way to his wedding. He would have liked to return the pretty belt to its owner, but not knowing whose it was, he put it in his saddlebag, as a present for his fiancée, and continued on his way.

Block gazed mournfully out of the cottage door and flicked the latch: tchack, tchack, tchack, on and on, until his mother caught him a blow across the back of the head. "Make yourself useful and shovel me some snow!"

Out of the snow she built a figure – less dumpy and more curvy than most snowmen. When it was finished, it could have been Florimell's twin! It was a comfort – a compensation for her boy – rather like the King of the Sea showering his son with treasure to make up for a life without love.

Block would have settled for marrying his 'Snowy Florimell'. But he took her out for a walk one day, sat her down somewhere, then forgot where and came home without her. His mother should have attached her by a cord to Block's cuff, as she did with his gloves.

The boat was not built for the open sea. The boards were rotten. Soon rain and spray beat into it too, filling it half full of slopping water. Every mountainous wave threatened to stand the boat on end and tip Florimell into the grey sea. Her cries of terror were snatched from her lips by a bitter wind, and her prayers drowned out by thunder and the loud swash of the sea. *"Help! Oh, help me someone!"*

Down in the ocean where all Life began, the god Proteus cocked his head. Preparations were underway for a great feast, but amid the cacophony Proteus picked out the high note of a woman's scream...

As the little rowing boat disintegrated into planks, Proteus caught Florimell by her hair and pulled her aboard his chariot, carrying her down to the ocean bed. The touch of her warmed his clammy hands. Her beauty brightened the deep lightless places. Proteus stared into her frightened face and liked what he saw. He liked it very much. Even wet and bedraggled and afraid, Florimell was lovelier than all the sea nymphs and mermaids. As a collector of beauty, Proteus wanted to own her.

"No!" cried Florimell (not for the first time that day). "My heart was given to Marinell and my heart died with him! I have no love to give you!"

"I'll settle for some kisses," said Proteus licking his salty lips.

"Oh no, no!" protested Florimell. "My love for Marinell is totally pure!"

"Down here everything is dilute," said Proteus.

"No, no! You will never sway me!"

"Down here in the tide-rips everything sways... or else it breaks," said Proteus, ugly now with menace. "Rest here while you rethink your answer!" And he locked her into his deep-sea dungeon, a place of slime and sea slugs and blind, white crabs.

Meanwhile, in chambers lit by glimmering plankton, the Sea Healer was working deepwater magic. He stitched up the wound in Marinell's chest, distilled dark liquors to pour between the boy's pale lips, snatched him back from the brink of death. "How can I ever thank you!" cried Cymo. "You have saved my son!"

But all this passed unnoticed in the booming busyness of Neptune's palace. Much greater events were afoot – a marriage between two rivers. The Medway and Old Thames came coiling down to the seashore, their watery trains dragging through a hundred miles of countryside apiece. They came bearing gifts for their wedding guests – salmon fry and clay, acorns and leaves, otters and sweet spring water. All this they tumbled into the sea, tingeing its colour with colours of their own. Their marriage was celebrated within the Halls of Neptune, with feasting, music and general humptidoodle.

Marinell was well enough to see the wedding preparations. But being a mortal, he was not invited. Indeed, when he reached out to take some of the delicious seafood, his mother slapped his wrist and sent him packing.

So Marinell wandered off to explore – down trenches and passageways, through bedrooms and antechambers, through kitchens and sculleries where custards and soups bubbled in great turtle shells, along lonely unlit lanes and on down into the dank, dark cellars.

The sounds of the party faded to nothing behind him. There was no noise but the sobbing echo of a woman whispering aloud to herself, trying to keep up her courage in the dark: "Oh Marinell! If only there had been time! If only you could have known before you died how much I loved you! Oh Marinell, what do I care if I must die? My world is empty without you! How can Proteus hurt me any more than I am hurting already?"

Astonished to hear his own name, Marinell peeped through the bars of Florimell's prison cell.

And there she was!

He opened his mouth to speak: he was within a breath of speaking… but he did not. All his young life he had been taught to live alone. He pitied Florimell with all his heart and soul. He loved her sweet face! But the Prophecy! The Prophecy! How could he ignore the Prophecy? Does a boy cram his mouth with nuts when he knows nuts will kill him? The man to whom sunlight is fatal – does he strip himself naked at noon? Consumed with a million regrets, Marinell ran back the way he had come. His cheeks were feverish, his pulse galloping. His thoughts were a jumbled nonsense.

He said nothing to his mother. He did nothing to rescue the girl from the dungeons. He kept to the upper staterooms. He kept the oath he had long since sworn. His life depended on it after all...

Within hours he was gripped by fever. Within the day he was lying hollow-eyed on his bed. The Healer's magic was powerless to help him. As Old Thames and Medway were married and intertwined watery fingers in the great banqueting hall, young Marinell lay below, losing the fight for life.

"What is wrong, son? Tell me!" his mother pleaded.

"I would if I understood, Mother," whispered Marinell. "I kept my oath and still I'm dying." And he explained about the girl in the dungeon and his struggle not to love her.

Cymo went directly from her son's room to Neptune, King of the Sea. In front of his throne she fell to her knees. "O Neptune, help me! Tell me what to do! Advise a foolish, frightened woman at her wit's end..."

Florimell looked up in fear as keys rattled in her cell door. But there, in place of her tormentor, was the Lady Cymo.

"Come child," said Cymo. "My son needs you." And she led the way through coral mazes to the chamber where Marinell lay. Florimell thought her heart would mend and break in the space of an hour. For Cymo showed her the beloved she had thought was dead – and there he lay, at Death's door.

Her tears woke him, splashing his face. He looked up at her in pure joy – glanced towards his mother, and promptly turned his face to the wall.

"No, no, son! Love her all you wish – with all your heart and soul!" Cymo insisted. "I was wrong to try and make you live without love!"

"But the Prophecy, mother...?" said Marinell, confused.

"The Prophecy has come and gone. The danger is past; I don't know how. But now you are free of it, and so is Florimell. It is time to obey the Laws of Love!"

Out of the blue, Florimell said, "Perhaps it was a maiden in disguise!"

"What was?" said Marinell. "Who?"

"The knight who wounded you. Perhaps it was a maiden in disguise!"

Marinell smiled and patted her little hand indulgently. "I think I can tell a maid from a man, my dear, ha ha ha!" he said.

And Florimell did not press the point.

❄ ❄ ❄ ❄ ❄ ❄ ❄ ❄ ❄ ❄

CHAPTER FOUR
Eat Your Heart Out

BRITOMART — THAT WOMAN in knight attire — knew nothing of all this. She continued her search for Artegall whose face she had seen and loved in the magic glass. She did meet Sir Scudamore, though — the elfin knight who had killed the witch's pet monster on the seashore.

Seeing a pall of smoke in the distance, Britomart rode towards it and came in sight of a castle. The castle itself was not on fire, but simply circled round by a hundred-hand-high hedge of flapping flame. Riding closer, she found Sir Scudamore slumped down in his saddle, weeping piteously. "My dear one! My darling!" he was wailing. "How can I ever save you?" There was panic in his voice and there were scorch marks on his shield. His horse's mane had been burned off short. Clearly he had tried more than once to break through the fiery barrier.

"What's wrong?" asked Britomart. "What place is this?"

"It's the castle of that villain Busirane! He has kidnapped my lady Amoret! He has her in there and what can I do? Nothing!" Scudamore drove in his spurs one last time but his horse only shied away, eyes rolling, hooves slipping on the cobbles. "We were to be married! We were marrying! The service had begun. The organ was playing. Our friends and families were all there! Suddenly so was HE, with his ropes and chains and fast horses. He snatched her from under our noses! My wife! My Amoret!"

Britomart leaned over and touched him gently. "Is he holding her to ransom, or what?"

"Ah, God alone knows! But she's not the first. People fear him worse than quicksand in these parts… Oh Amoret! What is he doing to you?"

Britomart dismounted, took the magic spear from her saddle and tucked away a wisp of golden hair under her helmet. Then, trusting to the power of Pure Love, she stretched out her lance… and walked into the fire.

It was like walking through a waterfall. The sparks were sharp as rose-thorns, but she did not burn. The flames divided and closed up behind her, their roar filling her ears. The flames did not lick her face or melt the metal of her armour. Even the plumes of her helmet were not singed. Though Britomart did not realise it, her pure love for the knight-in-the-mirror burned hotter than any sorcerer's magic; the fire-hedge was powerless to hurt her.

She could not hold the curtain open, though, for Scudamore. There was no choice but to enter the Castle of Busirane alone. The weather was worse on this side of the fire-hedge; the air was thick with thunder. Dire rumblings, like the beat of a great drum, shook the earth under her feet and fetched mortar from between the rose-red stones, but no guards challenged her. A notice on the door before her read: BE BOLD.

Britomart took her courage in her hands and pushed wide the door. She found herself in a great hall carpeted in red and hung with scarlet tapestries. Even its ceiling was crimson. The hall was empty. She walked the whole length of the room, watched only by the portraits on the walls, past empty chairs pulled up to a bare table. She called down side passageways but was answered only by her own echo.

On each door she came to were those same words: BE BOLD. She obeyed, sword half drawn, chin jutting, expecting, as she opened each door, to come face-to-face with Busirane. The windows darkened and night fell outside, though lightning flashes still showed her each empty room, its furniture seared white as bones. The whole building seemed to quake and pulse around her – a red heart pumping her through its valves and chambers.

At last she came to a door on which the words read differently:

BE BOLD… BUT NOT TOO BOLD

OR ELSE YOUR LIFE-BLOOD SHALL RUN COLD.

Britomart mustered not only her courage but all her common sense as well. Silently she opened the door just wide enough to slip inside.

There stood the sorcerer in front of his prisoner. He had bound the lovely Amoret to a pillar and wound around them both a cocoon of luminous magic. Without need for a knife, without making a wound, he had plunged his hand into her chest and taken hold of her beating heart!

You see, Busirane fed on Love. His life depended on it. Only Love could satisfy his ravenous hunger. Only Love fuelled his wicked magic. His whole scarlet house was heated by passion; it pulsed to the rhythm of a thousand racing hearts.

For a moment, Britomart froze with horror. Busirane turned towards her, face as whitely blank as a drowned man's. Moonlight and lightning poured in at the window. Then he stepped towards her, Amoret's heart in one hand, the other reaching, clawing. He was not fooled by her disguise: his sorcerer's eyes saw through to her woman's pulsing heart, and his hand groped greedily. His nails scraped the metal of her breastplate. White against black, snow against pitch, her magic was pitted against Busirane's. But Busirane had not had time to eat his bloody nightly meal, and Britomart had come armed and forearmed. She struck out at Busirane, piercing his spidery cocoon of magic and felling him to the ground.

She would gladly have killed him, then and there. But the words on the door rang in her memory: OR ELSE YOUR LIFE-BLOOD SHALL RUN COLD. And she turned her blade aside from Busirane's throat. She must not let Hate stain her quest for Pure Love. "Get up, Busirane," she said. "Replace that heart you hold in your hand. Then you have prisoners to set free."

"Thank you, thank you, sir knight!" the ladies cried as Britomart unlocked their cell door. Some tweaked at their hair and glanced shyly up at Britomart through their lashes, thinking him very handsome indeed.

Amoret was more grateful than any, but her heart was loyal to Sir Scudamore. "I thought it would be him. I thought Scudamore would come for me…"

"He did. He is outside waiting," said Britomart, pushing Busirane into his own dungeon and slamming the door.

Amoret fairly ran through the castle; her skirts caught up in both hands. The other silken ladies rustled along behind, pattering out into the castle's courtyard, hardly daring to believe they were free at last. Their hearts had been sucked dry of love… but love regrows, given time and sufficient tenderness.

As for Britomart and Amoret, they raced each other towards the castle gates. "Scudamore truly is outside?" gasped Amoret.

"Waiting to take you home."

Beyond the moat-bridge, the hedge of fire had blown out like a candle. Smuts of ash still hung in the morning air, but of the magical barrier there was nothing left.

Scudamore too was gone.

"Why?" said Amoret, her hand to her aching heart.

"I'll help you find him," said Britomart, laying a hand on Amoret's sleeve.

But Amoret snatched her arm away and shot her rescuer a doubting glance. What would the world say — what would Scudamore say if he knew she was travelling the world alone in the company of a strange young man?

Without stopping to think, Britomart took off her helmet in the hot midday sun. Amoret stared at the long, golden hair spilling down around the lovely face that had never worn a beard.

"Oops," said Britomart, blushing. "You mustn't worry. I am quite good with a sword. And I have a magic lance, so I can probably keep us both safe… You see, you are not the only one searching for your heart's desire." And she told her story — of the magic glass — of falling in love — of her quest for Love and a happy ending.

Amoret listened delightedly. Her honour was safe! She was travelling with a woman! Scudamore would have nothing to reproach her with, when they met up again. Better still, she had found a friend, and when trouble looms, there is nothing so vital as a true friend.

"I hear there's a wedding tournament being held near here," said

Britomart. "If Artegall is in the neighbourhood, he is sure to enter."

"Of course! Scudamore, too!" exclaimed Amoret. "How clever of you! Do let's go there! Oh, to see his dear face again!"

"Oh to see my one's face at all," said Britomart and smiled sadly to herself.

❋ ❋ ❋ ❋ ❋ ❋ ❋ ❋ ❋ ❋ ❋

Chapter Five
Winners and Losers

"SHE IS WHAT?" said Scudamore.

"Gone, yes," said Duessa, nodding and smiling. "With that handsome young knight. Sorry to say it, but your sweetheart seems to have thrown you over in favour of her rescuer."

First Duessa had lured him away from the Castle of Busirane with talk of dragons and damsels in distress. Now, she was telling him she had seen Amoret riding off knee-by-knee with Britomart. Scudamore could not take it in. He looked like a man who has come home to find his house burned down.

And yet why should this lady lie?

The evil Duessa smacked her lips. She loved the taste of lies; they lay so sweetly on the tongue. And to have her revenge on Cleopolis, she would spit lies in the eye of every elfin knight in Faerie Land. "I myself am in need of a protector, sir," she lisped, stroking his sleeve.

Scudamore nodded glumly. He did not want a new sweetheart so soon after losing the old one, but he could not refuse a direct request from a lady. It would not be chivalric.

A tournament draws people to it like high ground in a flood. When a tournament was mounted to celebrate the marriage of Florimell and Marinell, everyone within ten miles made their way there to watch or fight or sell refreshments to the crowd. Pennants fluttered and pavilions strained at their guy ropes. Farriers shoed horses and armourers riveted home cheek-plate and grieve. Squires practised their swordplay on each other. Unattached ladies combed their hair, hoping to catch the eye of some unattached knight.

Among the combatants were several knights errant from the Court of Cleopolis, several from the Borderlands, too. Some came from Albion and even far-off Lyonesse. Soon the grass on the field of combat had been mangled by countless hooves; the surgeon was tending to rows of wounded men. Horses stood creamy with sweat amid clouds of steam. Broken swords and split helmets littered the lists, and the tiltpoles sagged askew. Pages were brawling, and the last few undefeated knights drank thirstily to wash the dust out of their throats.

Sir Scudamore, believing Amoret had betrayed him, cared so little for his life just then that he fought with reckless, angry bravery. He seemed bound either to die or to win outright… until the arrival of the Scruffy Knight.

This Scruffy Knight was like some garden flower that has blown over the hedge and run to seed in the hedgerow. The chin below his visor was unshaven and his surcoat was ragged. His horse had not been groomed nor his saddle polished, and long tendrils of ivy clung to his shoulders where he had ridden through forest. Mud obscured his coat-of-arms, too. When he swatted Scudamore out of the saddle, like fly off meat, the crowd buzzed with guesses as to who this Scruffy Knight might be.

Scudamore had no sooner been carried away on a stretcher, to have his wounds tended, than in rode a young knight accompanied by a woman of extraordinary loveliness. The knight was Britomart (hair tucked up and hidden once more) and at her side was Amoret.

"Has a knight come here, by the name of Scudamore – an elfin knight – a knight errant of Cleopolis?" asked Amoret of a woman in the stands.

She could not have picked a worse person to ask.

"No one of that name," said scheming Duessa. "No Scudamores here."

"What about a knight called Artegall?" asked Britomart. Her heart beat faster just holding the name in her mouth.

Duessa smiled. "Nah."

But the Scruffy Knight had overheard the question. "If you are in search of a knight to fight you must settle for me!" he called.

Britomart began to protest. "Oh, but I did not come here to compete! I just came looking…" But the Scruffy Knight was already bearing down on her. There was nothing for it but to fight. Like half a hillside, the Scruffy Knight came on, tangled locks and unkempt beard hiding his features, scraps of moss flying from his horse. A strong smell of sweat and other people's blood came with him.

A lesser heart would have quailed, but Britomart was merely irritated. Could men not even manage to hold a conversation without resorting to swords and maces and pikes? She levelled her magic lance and prised the Scruffy Knight out of his saddle like a cork out of a bottle.

"A CHAMPION! WE HAVE A CHAMPION!" declared the Master of Revels, while the crowd cheered and the ladies in the stands leaned over the rail to ogle Britomart. "Choose your prize, stranger! All the ladies you see before you are heart-free and well born. Each one is offering a purse of gold to have you for her champion!"

"Argh! No thank you!" said Britomart in a panicky rush. (Win a lady? It would be like winning a pig at the fair and just about as useful.) She caught Amoret's eye and they both dissolved into silent giggles.

Then Britomart and Amoret rode away, leaving the Master of the Revels confused, the ladies disappointed, Duessa gloating, and Scudamore still resting in the tents, unaware that his loving lady had come and gone.

As for the Scruffy Knight, he was raging with resentment. He had never been unhorsed before not in all his knightly days! Never! Somewhere, somehow he must catch up with that insolent little knight and demand a rematch. Until then, his pride would burn like an open wound.

He had no idea he had just met his Fate, the other half of his soul. But then neither did Britomart. She had been quite unable to recognise, under his grubby disguise, Sir Artegall, the Face in the Glass.

❋　❋　❋　❋　❋　❋　❋　❋　❋　❋

CHAPTER SIX
Shaggybag

ALL THIS WHILE, Timian was moving through a living dream. Honeysuckle tangled his ankles, lilies collided with his hands, peaches brushed his mouth and gauzy sunlight blurred his sight. Or so it seemed to Timian.

Cured of his wounds, fed on a heady salad of herbs and healing flowers, he trailed now in the wake of Belphoebe the Huntress, lost in adoration of her. Never had anyone so sublime stooped to show him such kindness. She was magnificent in her green faerie glamour. The hair piled up on her head was like sunlight breaking through the crown of a tree. Her hunting robes clung to her form like ivy. When she drew back her bowstring, Timian felt his spine flex. Oh to be the bow in her hands! The bracken under her feet! The rain falling on her face! Oh to be the little pet dove that perched on her shoulders like some tiny spotless angel! Timian was bewildered by joy. He barely gave a thought to his master or the quest they were supposed to be pursuing. He had fallen into a crack in Time, like a grain of wheat into the ground, and Belphoebe was drawing him back up into the sunlight!

Not that she loved him, of course. Ladies like Belphoebe don't love boys like Timian, he knew that. Enough that she smiled on him, let him fetch back her arrows and wax her bowstring!

Then, the day after the Tournament, another person's love story spilled over into his, and nothing was ever the same again.

Amoret and Britomart were sleeping on the forest floor when Shaggybag came galumphing along. Despite the flapping of huge elephant ears, the scraping of tusks among the leaf-litter, Britomart did not wake. The hairy arms coiled around Amoret, squeezing her so tightly that she could not catch her breath or cry out. Only the sound of running feet woke

Britomart in time to see Shaggybag disappear into the forest carrying her friend.

For all his elephant looks, Shaggybag was no vegetarian. He preyed on tender young women – the younger and tenderer the better – storing them live in a damp dark cave before eating them without even the good grace to use a knife and fork. A stone blocked the cave mouth, and as he set Amoret down to open his larder, she gathered up her skirts and ran.

She ran her fastest, but Shaggybag was no lumberer. He was as huge and as fast as a charging elephant. As he closed on her, his hairy, lumpen nose snuffled in her ear, his tusks grazed her ribs, his forehead struck her in the back and then she was off the ground, cradled in those monstrous tusks.

Her scream dislodged a hundred birds from the branches overhead. The acorns fell from the paws of a dozen squirrels.

Timian the Squire, gathering feathers to fletch Belphoebe's arrows, also heard the scream. He looked round and saw Shaggybag come trampling through the wood. Drawing out his short-sword, Timian threw himself in the path of the brute, mindless of the risk from those curved boar tusks. As he thrust out his sword, the monster swung its prisoner over his shoulder, clasping her close to his hairy chest, using her as a human shield!

Timian tried to turn aside his stroke, but his blade nicked the girl's body before catching Shaggybag a glancing blow. The knowledge paralysed him. He had wounded a woman! The sight of the brute's filthy black blood staining Amoret's white dress held him mesmerised. Shaggybag recovered himself and, hugging his captive's limp body in front of him, kicked Timian aside.

"We meet at last, vermin!" shouted a high, clear voice. Belphoebe, her bow at full stretch, stepped from between the trees. At the sight of her, Shaggybag let out a harsh, demented bellow. He recognised his Fate as plainly as if it were written on Belphoebe's golden browband: DEATH. He tried to hide behind Amoret's body, but the arrow struck him in the throat and he was dead before his elephant ears had stopped flapping.

Belphoebe calmly unstrung her bow, glancing back along the forest path at those she had rescued. Timian had drawn Amoret's head into his lap.

"I'm sorry! I'm so sorry!" he wept, letting his tears fall into her closed eyes. "So beautiful! So young and so beautiful! And I cut you with my sword!

I let that fiend's blood stain you! Oh please don't die! Don't die, my lady!" In his sorrow and remorse, he actually bent and kissed her eyes, her mouth, the hair made tarry by the monster's blood.

"So," said Belphoebe, her voice prickly as hawfrost. "I see you have found another altar to worship at. No sooner are you healed than you are off hunting the heart again."

"Oh no, I..." Timian was appalled. "You are all the world to me, Belphoebe!"

"And yet you spend your kisses on another."

"Oh no, I... It's just that I..." She turned away. He squirmed to his feet and ran after her, but she had restrung her bow and turned on him, stamping her foot, aiming an arrow at his breast.

"Go," she said. "I have done with you."

"He's mine," said Scudamore dragging his sword from its sheath.

"I saw him first," said Artegall reaching for his.

Ever since the tournament, they had been travelling about together. Now they saw Sir Britomart galloping towards them along the path.

"That jackanapes stole my lady from me!" protested Scudamore.

"Yes, but he knocked me out of the saddle and no one has EVER done that before!" snarled Artegall.

Both were bent on revenge and neither was in the mood to parley. Britomart saw that at once. She had been going to ask them to help look for Amoret – poor stolen Amoret – but instead she saw she would have to fight both men before either would listen.

Artegall's pride was stinging and his blood was up. Britomart put up a good fight: she was light on her feet and had sparred with her brother too many times to go down at the first clash of sword. Artegall though had the strength and stamina of a true knight and not just any knight. He was a champion of Queen Gloriana herself. At last, with a sudden ballestra he drove her on to her back foot and unbalanced her. His sword sliced at her head and her helmet was cleaved in half. The two halves fell cleanly away, letting Britomart's golden hair tumble down.

When winged Pegasus clipped the top of Mount Olympus with one hoof, myth says that luscious wine ran down from the crack. In the same way, Britomart's long golden hair spilled down over her shoulders, over her breastplate, over her upraised hands.

Artegall stared. He took off his helmet and wiped the sweat from his eyes, the better to see. That was when Britomart recognised the face in the magic glass. "You are Sir Artegall," she said.

"You are beautiful," said Sir Artegall as if the words had never been said before by anyone anywhere.

Golden Arthur finally tracked down his squire when he came across a tree carved with the name 'Belphoebe'. Every tree for a furlong seemed to have the same carving: Belphoebe. Lying in the grass nearby were Timian's sword and dagger, discarded like broken cutlery.

Knocking at a ramshackle hut, Arthur was confronted by his one-time squire, though they barely recognised each other. Hollow-eyed, whey-faced and thin as string, Timian looked at his master dully. "I wish I were dead," he said.

"Ah! Unrequited love," said Arthur sagely. "Come home, Timian. You cannot go on living here, like the woodcutter in a bad fairy tale. Come on! The Future awaits! To Cleopolis and the Faerie Queen!"

But Timian only repeated, "I wish I were dead."

"A squire should serve his knight. It is his duty. We are on a quest, remember?" said Arthur pushing past into the hut. Inside, he found Amoret recuperating from her ordeal. Lifting her gently, he told Timian to fetch his belongings. Timian only stared at the wall. "I wish I were dead."

Arthur sighed heavily. "Despite what people say, Timian, True Love is not an arrow. Arrows only fly one way. True Love is a bridge – solid and strong. It is crossed in both directions. Your love for Belphoebe is a wonderful thing – a selfless thing – a sweet rapture. But the best love songs are duets. Amoret here and her husband. Sir George and the Lady Una. You will always love Belphoebe: nothing and no one can stop you. But one day, when you are older, someone may love you, Timian. And for that to happen you must be someone worth loving – a squire, a bold quester! A man. Here – take this ruby. Give it to Belphoebe, and tell her you will love her forever, but that you are leaving now – leaving to do your duty." And with that he plucked one of the rubies from his breastplate and pressed it into Timian's frail, trembling hand.

Sir Scudamore, Britomart and Artegall were still searching the woodlands for Amoret when the golden figure of Arthur came flashing through the trees. From behind his golden helmet, a woman's hand was waving and a voice was calling: "Scudamore! Scudamore my love!"

The tournament was over but the feasting was still in progress. Retracing their steps, the party of questers rejoined the wedding celebrations of Marinell and Florimell.

"Oh, I quite forgot!" said Scudamore as they sat down to eat. "I have a present for you, dearest Amoret," and he fetched from his saddlebag the belt he had found on the beach.

The bride, seated at the head of the table, caught sight of the belt and exclaimed, "Oh! But that's mine! I dropped it when I was running away from the witch!" Embarrassed, Scudamore at once rose to return it to its rightful owner. "Oh no, I didn't mean… Keep it, please! It was just the surprise of seeing it again.

Give it to your lady, by all means… But I should just mention, sir, that it carries an enchantment. It will only stay latched around the waist of a pure-hearted woman." She said it shyly, modestly, not wanting this to sound like a boast.

"What? Have I arrived at present-giving time? Well, look what I found in the wood!" crowed a shrill voice from the doorway. "Perhaps I have a present the bridegroom would prefer to the one he has got!"

It was Duessa, and on her arm, gliding through the crowd like an ice skater, came… Florimell! Another Florimell, identical to the first.

Marinell stared. Which was the true Florimell? Duessa snickered, and rubbed her hands with glee. What a shambles this would make of the happy wedding!

"This is easily settled," said Artegall briskly rising from his seat. He considered himself a man with a knack for settling arguments. "Let them both try on the belt!"

Duessa chivvied her companion up on to the banqueting table. There she stood, between the wedding cake and the custards, looking down into Marinell's face – a beautiful, silent, woman with ice-cold feet. Artegall passed her the pretty belt. She wrapped it around her hips and a smile spread across her lovely face – then beads of sweat, then a trickling blankness as she began to melt. Not so much false in heart as a forgery from head to foot, Snowy Florimell melted away within the magic circle of the belt, leaving only a wet patch on the tablecloth.

Artegall picked up the belt and gave it back to the true Florimell – true in every sense of the word.

As he returned to his plate, Sir Artegall asked yet again of Britomart, "Now will you marry me?" Every night and every morning, every hour and every mealtime since they had met, he had asked. So far Britomart had not replied.

"With all my heart," said Britomart now, as if there had never been any other answer possible.

"I have still to make my Festival quest for the Faerie Queen."

"I shall wait for you."

"How long?" said Artegall.

"For ever," said Britomart, "though I'd rather it didn't take that long."

Book Five
~
Artegall Rides Out
in the Cause of Justice

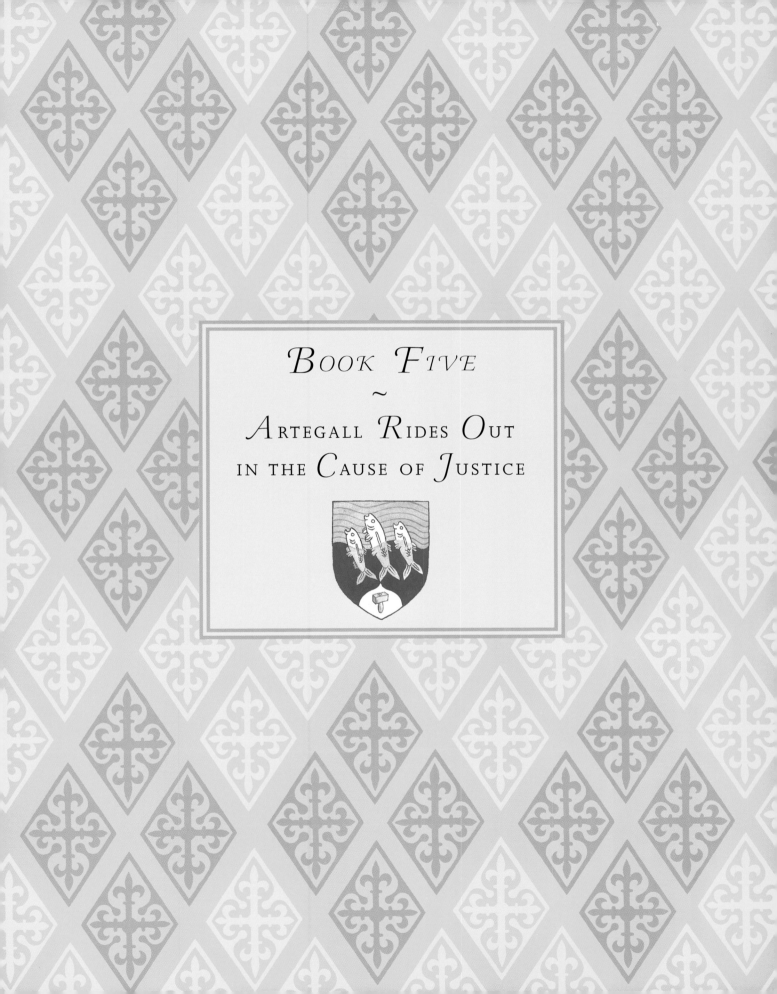

Chapter One
Blind Justice

There is one man at Cleopolis who is never troubled by the pangs of love – or even by indigestion. Talus feels no pain. But then Talus is not made of flesh and blood. Lucky Talus, some say.

When, at the Queen's Festival, Artegall recounted the story of Florimell's belt, it decided the nature of his quest. "You, Sir Artegall, shall ride out in the cause of Justice!" said Queen Gloriana. "You shall have Talus for your squire and enforcer, but first and foremost, *use your judgement.*"

Gloriana summoned Talus: a man of iron. He came lumbering into the Banqueting Hall now – a giant suit of armour brought alive and armed with a metal flail. *Clank, clank* went his steel knee joints and hips; *clatter, clatter* went the plates of his shoulder blades. But no heart beat inside his hollow chest. He was a man built to dispense Justice and not one tiny cavity existed in his metal body big enough to hold pity or clemency or doubt.

Artegall was well pleased with his assignment. The possibility of failure never once entered his head.

He and Talus were still within Faerie Land when they came to a bridge over a river. A man on horseback barred their way: "Stop and pay the toll!"

"A toll? What for? The upkeep of the bridge?" said Artegall.

"For the upkeep of my daughter," said the rider, with a smirk. "She has expensive tastes."

Artegall was angry. He had heard tell of officials demanding bribes, ferrymen robbing their passengers – but never before had something like this happened to him. "What if I don't pay?" he asked.

"Then I'll cut your throat and you won't be the first or even the fiftieth."

That made up Artegall's mind. He drew his sword and dug in his spurs. His stallion clattered on to the bridge.

Suddenly a trap door opened under him, and Artegall was plunged, horse and all, into the rushing river below.

The highwayman should have stayed on the bridge and watched Artegall drown, but in his bloodthirsty joy, he too jumped down through the trap door. He was used to fighting in water and, what is more, his horse knew how to swim.

Artegall did the only thing he could and grabbed him by the collar, hanging on, while both horses were swept from under them. They struggled above and below water until the highwayman began to tire and tried to clamber out up the bank. Artegall was behind him, sword in hand.

Talus stood waiting on the bank. Oil oozed from his ankles, like sweat, rust-proofing the hinges of his wet feet. His eyes were twin holes, iron filings for lashes. He flexed the hollow pipes of his twelve fingers...

Minutes later, the highwayman's body floated downstream, staining the water red, as his murders had done countless times before. Artegall squelched up to the castle gate. It was shut. "Knock, Talus," he said, and the iron man beat on the gate with his flail, sending splinters flying.

A lady's face appeared at a high window, fatly overfed and very frightened. Recklessly she flung handfuls of coin out of the window. "There! There you are! Now go away!" But the greed for gold is a human failing and Talus was not human. He continued to hammer at the gate with his flail until the timbers splintered, the crossbar fell away.

Piles as big as bonfires of gold and silver filled the counting house... but the lady herself was nowhere to be seen. Talus moved with unhurried strides – *chunk, chunk, chunk*. The knurled screws on the side of his head whirled in search of sound. The holes in his no-face sniffed the air. He snuffed his way to a heap of coins and, plunging in his steel gauntlets, unearthed the highwayman's daughter like a mole from its molehill. She had hidden herself

Hence the wrestling match in the sand.

"I am Artegall, Bringer of Justice!" said Artegall grandly. "I will settle this! The sea took land from Bracidas and gave it to Amidas. This is a natural process and must, therefore, be just!"

"Told you so! Told you so!" Amidas jeered at his brother.

Artegall persisted. "In the same way, the sea awarded the treasure to Bracidas and Lucy. It is therefore his to keep."

Lucy flung her arms around Bracidas who kissed her fondly. Philtera begun kicking her new fiancé in the shins. And Artegall and Talus went on their way, looking for further disputes to settle.

Farther along the coast, a great host of people had gathered on the beach, listening with bated breath to a man addressing them from the cliff top. He was an immense giant, and held in his hand a pair of brass scales. "Everything!" he was saying. "I am going to weigh everything! Earth and sea, moon and stars, beasts and crops — everything! Then I shall divide it equally between mankind so that everyone has their fair share! I shall weigh fire against rain and heaven against hell — here in the twin pans of my scales! The problem with the world today is Inequality. See how the sea sends its waves to plunder pebbles from the land? See how fire eats up houses and trees? Kings and queens and noblemen say, 'This land is mine; these deer are mine to kill; these fine clothes are fit only for me.' But I say this land is for everyone and everyone has an equal right to its riches!" The crowd cheered and laughed, happy to hear someone tell them: "When I have my way, every man and woman will own an equal share in the Earth!"

Filled with indignation, Artegall cut a path through the crowd. "Sir! You are nothing but a Leveller! God made everything in exactly the right amount and shared it out in just the right way!"

"Nonsense, elf!" rejoined the giant. "See how the mountains have raised themselves up over the plains? Inequity! See how the trees tower over the flowers? Inequity! I'll tear down the mountains and use the rubble to fill up the mines and valleys till everywhere is level again! I'll take the wealth from the rich and share it out among the poor!"

"Ignorance!" said Artegall. "Folly! You Levellers think you know better than your betters! Look at you with your ridiculous scales! Ha! Can you weigh the wind? Can you weigh one word that comes from between your stupid lips? Can you weigh Good against Evil? This isn't Justice, this is rabble rousing! Do it, Talus!"

While Artegall had been speaking, Talus had approached the Leveller, until the twin giants stood cheek-to-cheek. Now, on command, the iron man barged the giant off the cliff. He fell on to the rocks below and lay there like a ship driven ashore by storms, broken and lifeless. The pans and beam of his scales lay beside him.

When the crowd saw what had happened, resentment stirred. They grabbed up weapons and lumps of wood and began to encircle Artegall menacingly. "He was going to make all men equal!" they shouted.

Artegall was alarmed. He did not want to use his sword on mere peasants – that would be demeaning. He did not want to turn and run – that would be shameful. So he sent Talus to discuss a truce.

Talus was not a man of words – indeed, with no mouth in his head, he could not even speak. All he could do was to mete out Justice. And Justice is seldom about Right and Wrong. It is more often about keeping things as they are.

So he whirled his flail and scattered the ragged army. Men, women and children bolted for holes and bushes to hide in. Artegall watched, nodding with satisfaction. Faerie Land was not ready for the giant's kind of Justice. If Artegall had his way, it never would be.

✳ ✳ ✳ ✳ ✳ ✳ ✳ ✳ ✳ ✳ ✳

CHAPTER TWO
Among Amazons

ARTEGALL RODE ON, stout-hearted and a little smug. Talus clanked along behind, cleaning seagull droppings off his shiny head with a stick. A short way along the road, they heard women's voices and sighted several hundred ferocious women in warrior dress: Amazons!

They were in the process of lynching a knight.

Artegall drew his sword and galloped downhill, then reined in his horse. What was he thinking of? It was not dignified for a knight to fight women.

He sent Talus to fight them instead.

Talus's flail scattered the Amazons like crows off a cornfield, and the rescued knight was left precariously perched on a log, a noose around his neck, thanking his rescuers. "You saved me from Death and Dishonour! They wanted me to serve that queen of theirs — Radigund! I tell you, it's a living hell in that lair of hers! Better to die than to submit to... that." He nodded in the direction of the Amazon castle. "There are knights held captive there who will never be able to hold up their heads again."

"Take me there," demanded Artegall. "My quest is to bring Justice to the Borderlands! If this unnatural woman is holding men captive, I must punish her and set them free!"

The prisoner looked as if he would rather run in the opposite direction, but Artegall insisted. When they stood at the base of the castle wall, he called up to the parapets, "Radigund of Amazonia! In the name of Gloriana, I summon you to single combat!"

After some moments, Radigund appeared, crustaceous with shiny armour. "And if I win, will you submit yourself to the laws of Castle Amazon?"

"If you will submit to Justice, if I win!"

Radigund called for her armour-bearer. She called, too, for her captive knights, so that they might watch. Up they came — not from the dungeons but from the kitchens where they had been scrubbing pots and washing clothes. Each wore a bonnet and frock, beribboned hair and starched white aprons. Artegall thought he had never seen such a tragic sight in all his life.

Such was his outrage that he thought to kill the Queen of Amazons in the first flurry of strokes. But Radigund was a seasoned warrior, strong and quick-witted. She fought with all the savagery of a dog pitted against a bear. Elegant swordplay gave way to weary slashing, the clumsy clash of steel on shield, the rasping of breath in dry throats. Not until Artegall landed a blow to Radigund's head did her legs go from under her. She slumped down, unconscious, and Artegall knelt to unlatch the helmet and lay bare her neck.

A flood of glossy hair fell loose across his hand – a hank of silky softness that startled his senses. He brushed it aside and saw Radigund's face – beautiful, composed and as sweet as Demerara milk. Was there not something in the Laws of Chivalry against beheading so lovely a woman?

The dark eyes flashed open. The dark hand flew out and seized Artegall's sword. In a single movement, Radigund was up. Caught off-guard, Artegall stumbled backwards, failed to find his footing, and fell. Then Radigund was astride him, pinning him to the ground. Talus started forward, but the warrior women quickly surrounded all three.

Talus carved himself an escape route through them (though they hammered his head and buckled his body). But Artegall he could not save. Nor the prisoner, whose lynching went ahead just as if it had never been interrupted.

Artegall was taken to the castle scullery and given a calico gown and Dutch bonnet, and put to work as a maid. Every other servant, cook, launderer and maid was a captured knight bemoaning his ghastly fate. Given his way, Artegall would have refused this desperate humiliation, and opted for hanging, but he had sworn to submit. Now he could only hope to catch cold and die, or prick his finger on a needle and bleed to death before anyone in the outside world knew what had befallen him. The shame of waiting at table, sewing baby clothes, washing smalls and dancing strip-the-willow in a calico frock was more gut-wrenchingly horrific than any dragon. Day and night, come-day-go-day, Artegall fervently wished to die.

Talus stood in front of the Faerie throne, his head under one arm and his kneecaps hanging around his ankles. One elbow was gone and there was an arrow wedged in his navel.

Britomart had been burning with impatience for Artegall's triumphant return. Now she would rather have waited a year – a decade – than learn Talus's news. With the three remaining fingers on one hand, the iron man wrote down what had happened. All Cleopolis shuddered.

"I shall go and free him," said Britomart, strapping on her swordbelt and screwing Talus's left ear back into place. "May I take Talus?"

Graciously Queen Gloriana inclined her head. She could have sent Sir George – Sir Guyon – Sir Scudamore – but she allowed Britomart to go, not wishing to deepen Artegall's shame.

Talus led the way. Mended and refurbished, with a new flail in his six-fingered fist, he took her over the highwayman's bridge, past the twin islands and the body of the fallen giant, to Castle Amazon.

"I am Britomart, betrothed of Sir Artegall! Come down, Radigund! In the name of Queen Gloriana, I summon you to fight in single combat!"

Radigund appeared, carapaced in silver. "And if you lose, your sweetheart is mine to do with as I choose!" she called down.

Secretly, Radigund had taken rather a liking to handsome Artegall. In fact several Amazon warriors had cast hungry eyes over his sprig-cotton shoulders, the hairy ankle peeping out beneath his petticoats. Now they mustered along the parapets to throw rubbish down on Britomart.

Trumpets heralded Radigund's arrival. Just as the lioness is more of a hunter than the lion, so Britomart and Radigund would fight more fiercely than any man.

Though Radigund had slain thousands and Britomart had slain none, they were equally matched in skill. Disciplined fighting soon gave way to hacking and hewing; blood ran down unchecked: each woman knew she was fighting for her life. At last, Radigund struck round Britomart's shield and cut deep into her shoulder. The wound almost robbed her of the use of her arm, but the pain robbed her of all caution. She launched a furious attack – Radigund went down – and this time Britomart was not moved by a pretty face or a flood of hair. Here was a woman who had systematically felled men like a logger felling trees – a stranger to pity, whose only motto was *kill or be killed*. So Britomart locked pity out of her heart, as she had locked Busirane into his dungeon, and she let the deathblow fall. After all, Artegall was relying on her.

As the Queen of Amazons died, the watching women warriors gave a great sobbing moan. Then havoc broke loose. A hundred Amazons descended on Britomart, but Talus barred their way. Ten and twenty and thirty he killed, until Britomart called out, "Talus! Enough! For Pity's sake!"

The iron man looked around at her out of his no-eyes. The tilt of his head said, *Pity? What is that?*

Britomart dared hardly look. She kept her eyes on the floor, trying not to glimpse her sweetheart's pinafore and frock, his long hair in curly bunches, his embroidery half sewn. "Your stitches are very neat, my lord," she said awkwardly.

"Your backhand slash is excellent," said Artegall. "I watched from the window." He was painfully thin, having eaten nothing during his dreadful ordeal. So, while he and his fellow hostages changed back into doublet and hose and recovered their strength, it fell to Britomart to set right the State of Amazonia.

Her tongue tucked firmly into her cheek with concentration, she penned new laws on vellum in ink as red as blood:

No woman must ever again decree the law (she decreed).

No woman must hold the power of life over her fellow men (she decreed, on pain of death).

No woman shall hold sway over a man, except in matters of Love.

No woman shall rule except when men are not available to do it better.

Reading over her shoulder, Artegall ticked her statutes one by one like a teacher checking homework.

"And what have you learned, my quester after Justice?" asked the Queen of Faerie Land, resplendent in indigo gossamer.

"That Justice must be firm and swift and bold!" said Artegall grandly.

"And what of Pity?" Gloriana asked. "And clemency. And forgiveness?"

"Justice must be pitiless — impartial as the sea! Pity blunts the blade of Justice!"

The answer did not seem to please Gloriana as much as it had pleased Artegall when he had rehearsed it. Odd. Apart from the business with the Amazons (which he had glossed over) he thought his quest had gone rather well. Of course it had taught him nothing he didn't already know, unless… "Oh, and I learned that God never meant women to hold sway over men!"

There was a sharp intake of breath. An elfin chamberlain choked. A lady-in-waiting swooned. The candle flames trembled on their wicks. Even Talus ground his iron teeth. "What? What did I say?" asked Artegall.

"Except in Faerie Land, of course," Britomart put in quickly.

"Oh! Ah! Ooo! Except in Faerie Land, of course," said Artegall bowing so low that his hat fell off at his feet.

Gloriana has not yet given permission for Artegall and Britomart

to marry. She says, as a Knight of Justice he still has things to learn. Of course, she may take pity soon, and allow the marriage… There again she may decide 'Pity blunts the blade of Justice', and make them wait.

Book Six
~
Calidore Rides Out
in the Name of Courtesy

CHAPTER ONE
The Blaring Beast

✤ *T*IMIAN DID COME to his senses. He did give the precious ruby to Belphoebe and set off to catch his master up. He vowed to place Duty before Love!

Peering ahead of him through the trees, he yearned to see that shining figure clad in gold. He told himself how lucky he was to be squire to such a master: one who had scorched his brand on history, overfilling it so that one century, one realm had been too small to hold him. He must hurry, before Arthur despaired of him, got himself another squire less selfish and self-pitying… "I should be ashamed of myself," thought Timian, and he was.

And the Beast scents shame. That is how it finds its victims.

As Timian cantered along thinking his thoughts, it came lumbering out of the wood: the Blaring Beast. Suddenly, it was on him, bellowing like an elephant, claws ripping the braid from his tabard, sinking its teeth into Timian. It only dropped him when his screams brought help hurtling down the forest path in the form of Sir Calidore. The look that passed between knight and Beast was that of bull and matador. *To the death*, it said.

Unknown to Timian, Sir Calidore had already been dispatched by the Faerie Queen to hunt down this Blaring Beast. It was to be his Festival quest, and wherever his travels had taken him he had seen the chaos the Beast wreaked.

He reproached himself now as he lifted Timian's head, looked over his injuries. "If only I had not stayed to hear about Sir Artegall's Festival quest!

If only I had come an hour earlier!"

Timian could not hear. The bite of the Blaring Beast is so dirty that the wounds quickly canker and fester. As he lay along the ground wondering if he would live or die, he had begun hearing voices in his head: *...neglected his duty... as if Belphoebe would look twice... fickle boy... never make a knight...*

Calidore wanted to go after the Beast, but he could hardly leave Timian to die of his wounds. So picking him up, he carried the boy at a run. There was a castle in the distance – he could find help there. But between Calidore and the castle ran a fast-moving river. The water swamped his boots and put him in danger of losing his footing. It was very cold. To his huge relief, an elegant couple on horseback came down the bank behind him and began to ford the stream. "Please! Sir! Madam! Help me, won't you? This boy has been bitten by the Blaring Beast! His wounds need tending! Help me get him across the river! If I can just reach that castle over there..."

The knight (whose name was Turpine) turned on Calidore a look of exquisite boredom and disdain. "What do you take me for, a ferryman? And if you do get to that castle, fellow, you will be on my private property. We discourage trespassers, don't we my love?"

"We do, oh we do," said his lady with a sniggering sneer.

Calidore was enraged. "Call yourself a knight? And you refuse to help a fellow knight – or even a wounded boy! Get down and fight!"

Turpine's top lip rucked. "I don't think so, do you Blandina? I don't think we need bother."

His lady snorted again, like a pig. "No need to bother, my love." And they forged on across the river, their splashing horses soaking both Calidore and Timian to the skin and muddying the ford.

Carefully, fearfully, Calidore felt his way, step by freezing step through the rushing water. He did not feel the cold: he was too angry. Not just discourteous, but a coward, too! Timian was a dead weight in his arms.

The weather was growing worse. There seemed to be no other building but the castle anywhere in sight. Calidore would have to swallow his pride and beg shelter. Turpine could hardly defy the age-old laws of hospitality.

Up in a cosy gallery lit by the cheery flicker of a bright log fire, Turpine and Blandina sat eating toast and quince jam. They heard Calidore below their window, calling for someone to open the gate… but only snickered into their mulled wine, making the liquor bubble and slop.

"Do you feel a draught, my little sherbet?" asked Turpine.

"I do. I do feel a draught," said Blandina and summoned a servant to close the shutters.

Outside in the rain, Calidore lay Timian under a bush and tried to shelter him as best he could. The night dragged by, a nightmare of shuddering cold and wet and worry. By morning, Calidore was exhausted.

Turpine, on the other hand, woke boisterous and in the mood for cruelty. "I believe we have trespassers on our land, Blandina my love."

"I do believe you're right, sugar stick. Turn them off."

So Turpine took down his hunting javelin, put on his cloak and rode out to hunt Sir Calidore as he might a fox or a boar.

Calidore's hands were dead from cold. His sword hung in a tree, out of the wet. The boy's head lay in his lap. When Turpine came galloping out of the morning mist, Calidore was powerless to defend himself. He could barely even make sense of what was happening.

Suddenly, out of nowhere, a naked man leapt clear across bush and squire and knight. Huge and mud-spattered, with leaves in his hair and matted dirt in the hairs of his sunburned back, the Wild Man reared up to his full height. A boar-spear glanced off his leathery hide. Otherwise, it would have impaled Timian.

Turpine peered at the Wild Man who had thwarted him, and recoiled with fright. He tried to ride him down, but the Wild Man grappled him out of the saddle. Scared out of his wits, Turpine took off and ran, arriving back at the castle stables before his horse.

The Wild Man turned to face Calidore and raised two ham-like hands. Calidore flinched. "Who are you?"

But when the Wild Man continued to draw circles in the air with both hands, Calidore realised he was mutely beckoning. At close quarters he had the sweet smell and colour of a compost heap – and he lifted Timian easily on his two hands. Calidore, with his chilled, cramped legs, had trouble even keeping up.

At last, they reached a crude shelter – no walls but a thatch of interwoven branches with a tedding of dry grass beneath. Ingeniously, the Wild Man lit a fire, picked herbs, and made a warming broth.

"How strange," thought Calidore, "to find such courtesy in a primitive creature and none in a so-called knight."

Next morning, the Wild Man carried Timian to a monk's infirmary where he could be nursed until the poison either spared him or ended his young life.

❋ ❋ ❋ ❋ ❋ ❋ ❋ ❋ ❋

Chapter Two
Troucing Turpine

"The Blaring Beast has killed me," groaned Timian. "I only wish I had served my master better while I lived… I let Arthur down. That's what people are saying. I hear them. Here, in my head."

The Abbot placed a cool cloth over Timian's brow. "Recovery comes from within, young man. I can use all the medicaments in the world, but unless you decide to live, you will most certainly die."

Meanwhile, the unlikely alliance of Sir Calidore and the Wild Man set out to punish Turpine for his discourtesy. Sir Calidore was fully recovered from his night in the rain and the Wild Man's broth had put new strength into him. When they reached Turpine's castle, Calidore draped a blanket over hunched shoulders and knocked on the gate. "Open sir, and give shelter to a wounded knight, for sweet mercy's sake!"

A servant came to the door. "Take yourself off. Sir Turpine says if you must die of your wounds, to do it some other place. The steps were only scrubbed last week. Oh, and take your gorilla with you."

Calidore and the Wild Man exchanged glances. "Fetch your master, serf! You are surely lying! I cannot believe any man would deal so with a brother knight."

The servant shook his head. "Better believe it, sir. I put the message nice, so as not to give offence. Master really said, 'Set the dogs on them'."

Hearing this, the injured knight at the door made a sudden and complete recovery, brushing the servant aside. Calidore stormed indoors, just in time to see Turpine fleeing up the stairs. "What? A coward as well as unchristian?" cried Calidore, taking the stairs five at a time. Turpine ran faster, a moan rising to a squeal in his throat.

They found him in the bedchamber, curled up between his lady's knees, eyes tight shut, hiding under her petticoats. "Don't kill me!" he whimpered. "You wouldn't kill a brother knight, would you?"

"I shall spare you," said Calidore, "on the condition you never again use the title of knight or carry a sword! Courtesy is the only hallmark of a knight, and you have broken every rule of Courtesy!"

When Calidore went back downstairs to the courtyard, there was no sign of the Wild Man. He had simply disappeared, like the berries from a tree when they have served Nature's purpose.

❄ ❄ ❄ ❄ ❄ ❄ ❄ ❄ ❄ ❄ ❄ ❄

Chapter Three
Calidore Among the Shepherds

Sir Calidore, on his ride back to the infirmary, heard crashes and snarls in the undergrowth and thought, "No time like the present!" This time, he would let nothing delay or side-track him!

But the Blaring Beast proved as elusive as ever. He found its spoor; he found the damage it had done, but still it evaded him.

Seeing a group of shepherds, Calidore decided to ask them if they had seen the Beast or its lair.

"Nothing of that kind, nowise and nowhere. None of us has seen no blarting beast," said a jolly shepherd in a straw hat. "You look 'ot, sir. Rest yourself, why don't ye?"

So Calidore sat down with them – a dozen shepherds and one shepherdess. Their bread tasted wonderful, their ale delicious, their music interchimed with the clonking of sheep bells. The more the shepherds talked, the better Calidore like them, and the longer he stayed, the more he hankered after their gentle, rustic life

Most of all, he hankered after the shepherdess.

Her name was Pastorell and she was a girl of clear-skinned perfection. (Being something of a snob, Calidore preferred to believe she was not really a shepherdess but a lady of high birth mislaid in the forest by noble parents.)

Only one shepherd was not welcoming. Young Corry saw the smiles that passed between Sir Calidore and Pastorell and instantly loathed the elf knight.

"Rain's a-coming," said the oldest shepherd, sniffing the trembling air. "Won't ye sleep under my roof tonight?"

It was nothing but a turf hut, and yet Calidore revelled in its homespun hospitality. What a life they lived, these people! They did not chase after fame or money or fashion, or exchange spiteful gossip! The sun told them when to get up and when to go to bed. Their days were fleecy-lined with sheep. They feared only wolves and scrapie. It seemed to Calidore that they knew the secret of a happy life.

It seemed to Corry that Calidore was a pesky interloper.

Corry had long thought of Pastorell as his fiancée (though strictly speaking he had never proposed). He seethed with sulky jealousy.

His quest forgotten, Sir Calidore allowed one golden day to stretch out into a summer. Every day he fell deeper in love with Pastorell, and she with him. And every day Corry hated him a little bit more.

The idyllic days seemed set to last for ever. But just as autumn was plucking bare the summer, so tragedy was preparing to strip Calidore of his happiness.

Brigands had moved into the area. The shepherds, owning next to nothing, thought themselves safe from such men. But the brigands had struck on a new brand of crime. Foreign merchants passing through the Borderlands were willing to pay a good price for fit young men or beautiful young women. Far across the sea, such captives could be sold for gold – as slaves!

One day, when Calidore was out hunting, the kidnappers fell on the shepherds like wolves on a flock. The old and frail they killed; the rest they dragged away, driving both sheep and shepherds ahead of them.

When Sir Calidore returned from hunting, it was to a lifeless hillside stained and scuffed by struggles. Appalled, he stared around him, but nothing moved – nothing but the wind puddling the grass, the clouds scudding like scattered sheep. Frantically he searched among the dead for Pastorell – but found only Corry – bloodstained, face-down… and weeping.

"So sudden! We never expected… They took Pastorell! She's dead! She must be dead! I tried to fight them, but one clubbed me and I fell… I don't remember. They must have left me for dead!"

Calidore said nothing, but went straight to the old shepherd's hut and buckled on his armour once more (though he hid it under a sheepskin coat). "If they are still alive, I'll find them," were his parting words to Corry.

"Wait!" said Corry. "I'm coming with you."

Two shepherds moving through an autumn landscape do not attract much attention. A herd of sheep, a chain of prisoners leave a trail of crushed grass. Corry and Calidore tracked the robbers until daylight failed and the trail petered out. "Let's ask those shepherds yonder if they have seen anything."

But wading through the grazing flock to reach the circle of men, Corry began to recognise a docked tail here, a nicked ear there... "Pssst! These are our sheep," he whispered. "We've found our brigands."

"Hoi, you!"

They had been spotted. Their grips tightened on their shepherd's crooks. They were hugely outnumbered.

"What are you? Shepherds?"

"Uhuh," said Calidore.

"So you understand sheep? Filthy stupid animals. Always wandering off. Can't abide 'em. You want work?"

"We'll tend youz sheep for you, zir," drawled Calidore, "if thatz what youz wantin'. All we'z asking is a bite o' zupper."

"Zupper, yez," said Corry.

And so they wormed their way into the band, and said nothing, but listened to every word.

There had clearly been some falling out between the brigands and their chief. Mutiny was in the air. "If he keeps her to his-self, shut up in that there cave, where's our share of 'er to come from?"

"We should kill 'im and sell 'er us-selves!"

"Couldn't we keep her and share her between us-selves?"

"She ain't gold and silver."

So! The chief wanted to keep Pastorell for himself, did he, and not sell her to the slave-traders? The men around the campfire were angry.

"I say the slavers will pay twenty pieces for a woman like that!"

"How d'you divide twenty by twelve?"

"I say we kill 'em both and eat 'em. I'm sick of mutton."

"I'll drink to that!"

Calidore and Corry stood by, like two simpletons, and counted sheep by moonlight, ignored by the robbers who squabbled and brawled and drank. It seemed an age before they were all sprawled asleep on the ground.

CALIDORE RIDES OUT IN THE NAME OF COURTESY

At the sound of snoring, Calidore took a sword from beside one of the sleepers. Then he and Corry tiptoed away to search out the treasure cave. They found it in the base of the valley, its mouth blocked by a makeshift log door.

"One! Two...!" breathed Calidore. And on the count of three, they made more noise than the Blaring Beast itself, hammering on the door, shaking sheep bells, yodelling and yelping till the brigand chief came running out, sword-in-hand. He was dead before he saw moonlight.

"Pastorell! Pastorell!" cried Calidore.

Out of the cave staggered two dozen shepherds, their hands bound in chains. Out ran Pastorell, wild-eyed with fright and hope and joy and anguish. Courteous Calidore, of course, refrained from taking her in his arms. Fortunately, Pastorell had not been taught courtly manners. She flung herself at him and, with her fingers tangled in his hair, covered his face in kisses like a child eating honeycomb.

Even Corry looked on with patience, knowing he had lost Pastorell to a man deserving of her love.

❋ ❋ ❋ ❋ ❋ ❋ ❋ ❋ ❋ ❋ ❋

CHAPTER FOUR
Return to Cleopolis

THE SHEPHERDS TOOK more with them than their flock. They lugged away all the swag out of the cave. (A shepherd's life may be sweet, but only with money enough to weather old age and cold winters.)

Returning home, they were all set to twine bridal wreaths for Sir Calidore and Pastorell, but the knight said no: "I am a knight of Cleopolis, and – horse or no horse – I am on a quest! I shall not be free to marry until I have defeated the Blaring Beast. When that is done, I'll come back for my little shepherdess!"

"I'm coming with you!" Into sight rode a slight figure mounted on a shaggy carthorse, scattering sheep as he clip-clopped over the fields. Timian the page had at last taken to heart the words of the wise old Abbot. Duty and adventure had prised him back from the brink of death. The Beast's poison had been purged out of him by the blazing desire to slay it. As Calidore climbed aboard the carthorse (borrowed from the monastery), there was no more talk of shame or despair or failure.

And whatever fears and regrets Pastorell may have felt as she watched them ride away, she did not try to stop them. After all, she knew she could not compete with the call of Duty or the magic of the Faerie Queen.

Through the gardens of great estates, through fairgrounds and market squares, through tiltyards and shipyards and courts of law, they tracked the Beast. They saw its countless victims, the ghastly damage it had done. At last the trail of havoc led to a monastery and, as they galloped nearer, they could hear the tocsin bell ringing in alarm.

The Beast was ramping through the cloisters and chapel, poking its head into each bare cell, turning and turning about in the nave, smashing and staining and snuffing out the pale glimmer of holy candle flames. But in blighting Holy Church, the Beast had taken one step too far!

Its rump overturned the altar table as it turned to face them. Its unfolding wings sent sepulchres and statues toppling. Sir Calidore drew his sword and charged the length of the aisle. The cavernous mouth opened to greet him. Venom and bile and acid splashed his shield.

That mouth was as wide as the gates of hell. Inside it, a thousand separate tongues licked and lolled – the forked tongues of snakes, the curly tongues of cats – of dogs, bears, whales and tigers! But worst of all were the human tongues, for they were all speaking – slandering, laughing and lying.

And the noise! Calidore was swamped by noise. His eardrums bled; his head filled with lies and rumour and libels and snide slurs about everyone from Abraham to Arthur, from the holy saints to Edmund Spenser. *"Even now the Lady Pastorell is making daisy chains with Corry the shepherd! How she enjoyed that brigand's kisses! Belphoebe likes kissing the boys, too. Even Gloriana..."*

"Enough!" Sir Calidore picked up the rope of the fallen chapel bell. "I do not believe you!"

"We do not believe one word of your filthy lies!" bellowed Timian. A little boyhood rhyme was dancing in his head: *Sticks and stones may break my bones, but words will never harm me.*

The Blaring Beast blinked and all its tongues fell momentarily silent. Quick as a wink, they bound the snout round with rope. Unable to speak, the Beast lost half its strength. They fetched chains, and wound them round the scaly legs. Never in all its days had the Beast been bound. It staggered and tottered, so sapped of energy that the knights were able to lead it out of the monastery like an old blind donkey.

Through cities and towns they led it, through fairgrounds and shipyards, and everywhere people came out of their houses and cheered to see the Blaring Beast silenced and subdued.

The elfin knights of Cleopolis bound it tighter still, and the magic of the Faerie Queen herself buried it deep in the earth. With luck, it will take a lifetime to dig itself out again.

"So, what did you learn from your quest, Sir Calidore?" said Queen Gloriana. Iridescent peacock wings fanned out behind her hair, like a ruff of Spanish lace. Above her throne, honeysuckle had given way to passion flowers.

"I learned not to put off till tomorrow what should be done at once," he confessed.

"And what did you learn of Courtesy?"

"That Courtesy is not the preserve of knights," said Calidore. "Without it a knight is no better than a Wild Man; and Courtesy makes a Wild Man fit to champion a queen. I found as much Courtesy among shepherds as among gentlemen." He paused as an image of Pastorell's face distilled in his thoughts

like crystals of sugar. "And I learned that there are sweeter lives than questing… But none so important, of course!" he added hastily.

"Then I dub you my Knight of Courtesy. Choose a horse from my stables. It will speed you back to Pastorell."

Calidore hurried out. Odd, but in recounting his quest, he had not mentioned Pastorell. So how…? He shrugged and ran to the royal stables.

Suddenly Gloriana put out her hand and touched a young squire on the cheek. "What do you say to that, young Timian?"

Timian blushed. "I don't know what you mean, Your Majesty."

"On your journey here, did you not find a sweeter life than questing?"

"I…"

"With Belphoebe the Huntress, perhaps?"

How could she have known that? It was impossible! Only Arthur knew, and Arthur had still not found his way to the Court of Cleopolis!

Then the light caught it – a ruby, shining in the Queen's flame-red hair. How could that be? How could the Faerie Queen be wearing the same ruby that Timian had given to Belphoebe? Unless…

Faeries are shape-shifters, after all. They can be here and there and everywhere. What if Gloriana and Belphoebe were one and the same: the one confined to Cleopolis by the duties of a queen, the other free to hunt and roam and play and love?

So Timian spoke up – even though he was only a boy – even though he was nothing more than a visitor newly arrived from the Realm of Albion by way of his master's dreams. "I think… I think that Love is the sweetest calling of all, Your Majesty. But when a man serves you, Duty and Love are two sides of the same coin."

Gloriana smiled and raised her Faerie sceptre. "Then it is time you became a knight…'

Timian was astounded. "But Majesty! What about the virtues of knighthood – Courtesy and Holiness and Justice and Friendship and, and…"

Gloriana laughed. "Those are the virtues a knight spends a lifetime questing after. If you had them all already, Timian, you would be the most perfect knight ever to put on spurs! Talking of which… when will he come, that Arthur of yours! Does he lack all sense of direction?"

And on those very words, the trellised doors swung wide, and a knight ducked beneath the lintel of the Banqueting Hall. Arthur of Albion was overlarge for the architecture of Faerie Land – head-and-shoulders taller than any elf knight. Across the heads of her courtiers, he and the Faerie Queen regarded one another. He brought with him the quality of a dream, in that the carpets heaved, the walls wavered, the candle flames curled like tongues in the act of singing, and the light took on the colour of joy. All the butterflies embroidered over the Queen's heart suddenly took off.

"You come at last! We have been waiting for you, Arthur of Albion," said the Queen. "You are the last to arrive."

"My journey here has been… eventful," said Arthur wryly. He looked around the room, inclining his head to the friends he recognised: Sir George, Sir Scudamore, Britomart, Timian. Then his eyes returned to the Faerie Queen like moths to a lantern. "I dreamed," he said.

"I sent that dream," said she, and the hangings billowed out from every wall and window.

Crossing the room, Arthur bent his knee in front of the honeysuckle throne, offering the sword hilt of Excalibur, offering his service, offering his heart. Unspoken words hummed in the air like bees swarming after nectar.

Then Time recovered its heartbeat, and Gloriana took hold of Excalibur. "On the strength of what my own knights have told me, I was about to dub your squire. I lacked only your approval. Say. Does he have the makings of a knight?"

Arthur smiled at his squire. "Timian has more courage and loyalty than any man I ever knew. The other virtues will follow in time."

"Then arise Sir Timian, Knight of Courage, Dreamer of Albion! Arise, and let questing cease for another year. My Festival is done." She touched her white brow, where red ringlets curled like thoughts. "The year's words are harvested and in store. There is nothing left but to dance!"

What must it feel like, that wand on your shoulder? Like a whistle too high to hear, a blade too sharp to feel, a flame too blue to see. It is the stroke of an axe and the touch of a moth.

Of course, we can be knights, you and I! If Timian can do it, so can we! Let them all come: the beasts and dragons and blaggards and sorcerers; the witches and sirens and wraiths! Let them buffet and bite me till I look like the coastline of Norway! We shall drive them all away to the dark side of the moon and make the world into a bower of bliss!

For her, we can do anything!